MURDER IN THE BROTHEL GARDEN

A Conner Miles Mystery

STEVEN D. MALONE

CONTENTS

THE HANDMAIDEN

Galveston 1925

HOW CAN A DUMB IRISH KID GET TIRED OF MONEY? BUT THERE I was, standing over a table that sagged under a pile of money. True, it was a cheap-ass table. And the dough was the nickels, dimes, and quarters from an army of slot machines spread all over our side of Broadway. Silver shoveled, lugged, piled, stacked and counted through about fourteen hours of each and every Sunday and Monday of my life.

Three of us nursed all those coins in what should have been the second bedroom of my dumpy walk-up. That table and two mismatched chairs were the only furniture. My long time buddy, Bobbie Lee Glover, sat, knees up, on the floor, head resting on his knees, eyes closed. Tony "Papa" Regelo, my erstwhile boss, the man I drove all over our end of Galveston siphoning off the take from the slots, sat scratching numbers on a pad with a nib of a pencil. Jesus, that man could do the math. A counting fool and one cunning, drunk, son-of-a-bitch. I stood next to the remaining chair sweating in the warm damp left by this afternoon's thunder shower.

The screened, opened, window that blocked any breeze did not prevent two moths and a dozen gnats from circling the lone naked light bulb jammed in the fixture on the ceiling.

I heard knocking on the door downstairs. Two quick ones followed by a third. The kid, Porky, so called not for being fat but for being Portuguese, stood guard out on the porch. That particular pattern meant friends were coming.

Papa looked up. "Check it anyway."

Bobbie Lee grabbed the .38 laying on the floor by his butt, stood, and slid the pistol into his waist. He stepped to open the door.

"Damn, it's Manny Dents," he said after a moment.

Damn is right. Manny Dents was muscle for the Beach Gang. My gang. Manny's nickname, Dents, came from the dents left in the floor by the skulls of his victims. No one wanted to get punched by Manny Dents. His steady, plodding tread up the creaking stairs thudded loud in my ears.

Manny came in the room all shoulders and knuckles. His dark, handsome, Italian head was hatless and he was in his shirtsleeves for the heat of the night.

"Evening, Papa."

"Manny." Papa returned. Manny wasn't all that fond of his nickname. Smart folks avoided using it in his presence. Not if they didn't want one of those dents in their floor.

"Howdy, Reb," Manny greeted Bobbie Lee. What other nickname would you get with Robert E. Lee Glover as a moniker?

Bobbie Lee nodded.

"Conner, you gotta come see Mr. Maceo," Manny said to me.

As I stood, not enjoying the cold sinking feeling in my gut. I heard Bobbie Lee groan.

"Nuttin' to worry 'bout, Reb. I got orders to bring him back here."

"Rose or Sam?" I asked. It made a difference. The Maceo Brothers were up and coming lieutenants for the boss of the Beach Gang, Ollie Quinn.

"Rose."

Damn. Bobbie Lee groaned again. Rose Maceo was definitely not the nicer of the two brothers.

Manny chuckled. "Now, Reb, Rose likes you Paddies. Conner'll be coming back."

"I ain't no Irishman," Bobbie Lee said.

"You're all the same to him," Manny returned. "Come on, Conner. I wanta chase some skirts 'fore midnight."

I took a step and, I promise you, my knees wobbled.

"Scared, Conner? I guess I'd be. But, you're with us, and Rose ain't got no beef with you. Swear. I got orders to bring you right back here after."

I followed Manny Dents, and slid into his shiny black Ford. He stopped at the front, gave it a quick crank, and the beast clattered to life.

Galveston was a new city back then. Well, twenty years old. I guess that's new for a city. New because, when I was barely walking under the live oak and pecan trees of east Texas, a bad-ass hurricane wiped the old town off the sand, or most of it. What we passed in the dark wasn't built until the city fathers piled eighteen feet of new sand behind their new seawall. Most of the seawall was Beach Gang territory. Most of the businesses catering to tourists were controlled by us back then. The Maceos owned many directly.

I expected to head down to the Seawall. Instead, Manny turned down Avenue M, heading west. Through the neighborhoods, dark save for the half-moon shining from east over the Gulf.

"Not heading to the Kit-Kat?" I asked.

"Still scared, Conner?"

"I don't think so. Not now," I said.

"Remember, it's Rose."

"You know, my old man used to take me fishing out in his little boat. Every once in a while I'd spot a moc. Water moccasin. Ornery bastards. Scared me down to my socks. I'd ask my ol' Pa, ain't you scared, Pa? He'd say, no, not scared a' no moc. He'd pause, then say, but I show 'em a whole heap of respect, I do."

Manny laughed out loud. "Gotta lot of respect for ol' Rose, huh?"

"I do. You know, it was Rose that plucked me off the hustle. Hustling nickels and dimes. He gave me a job hauling liquor."

"And now you're back hauling nickels and dimes."

"Yeah, but now I'm hauling them in piles."

"You know, I think I gotta agree with Sam and Rose. I don't guess you're a dumb Paddy after all."

"They said that?" I asked.

Manny did not answer.

We ended up in the driveway of a medium size house a couple of blocks off the Seawall. Like many of the homes built after the great hurricane, this one sat high atop a brick base, a study of apparent permanence. The substantial front porch was lined with four great columns holding up the roof, and its eaves were draped in gingerbread lattice. A lone, naked light bulb shined down on us.

Manny rapped three times on the door. A short, round man of middle years opened the door. The sneer of a smile never reached his eyes as he took a look at us. Manny he recognized. The door opened and my life changed.

Except for the cloud of cigar smoke, the front room could have been that of my great aunt Mabel. Plush and posh furniture, that certainly served its purposes during the Civil War, decorated with lace doilies. Pastel silks and crystal both shaded and glittered around the ponderous lamps. Graceful, lion-footed coffee and end tables edged or fronted the couches and chairs. Framed daguerreotypes of someone's family covered the pale print wallpaper.

Is it irony that is the strange joining of mismatched themes? If that is so and this might have been my old Aunt Mable's parlor, five pure gangsters, making that cloud of Cuban cigar smoke, draped themselves along the regal love seat and lounging chairs. And all of them stared at me.

I knew two of them. The Maceo brothers, Sam and Rose. They were up and coming underbosses.

Rose picked me off the streets a year ago and more, had me

hauling kegs of whiskey off of the Galveston beaches, then set me up with Papa Regelo's slots business. I owed Rose Maceo. And I liked Rose. He was affable and looked every bit the Italian barber he started life as. He spoke with a broken Italian splutter, mixed with a South Louisiana rumble, that resonate slur that seemed to start deep in the throat and rolled over the roof of the mouth. Rose was all about business and as ruthless as his chosen business needed to be. No one crossed Rose Maceo.

Sam was a different story. I knew him by sight but this was the first time I'd met him. Everything one would want in an Italian stage actor. Slim, chiseled good looks, open and warm smile, eager eyes always looking right into yours. Suave, smoothly gregarious. Not a woman in Galveston wasn't left breathless under his attention. Not a man in town did not like and admire him.

The others I didn't know. At least not at that time.

What is it about Italian gangsters that they found a way to seem informal and relaxed and somehow posed as if for a portrait? The bunch of them were smiling and staring. And there I was, standing in the middle of the floor trying not to seem scared spitless and not forgetting that the most dangerous man I knew stood right behind me.

I saw Rose Maceo shift his gaze over my shoulder to Manny. He arched an eyebrow. I couldn't see or even hear Manny respond.

"Go see Schwartz," Rose told him. He turned to the others.

"Boys, dis is da Conner. Conner, everybody." Rose gestured an introduction across the men sitting so poised, so comfortable.

"Conner," they said, almost in unison.

"Everybody," I returned.

"Conner," another voice. A woman's voice.

I hadn't noticed her standing in the corner to my left. She was a wreck in flapper clothes. Shiny onyx hair, disheveled as if fingers had run through it. Nice skin the color of piano keys. Might have had pretty, dark eyes, but tears blotted her mascara and ran down her cheeks.

I gave a quick nod. She looked away. If I have ever seen a spent woman, there she stood.

"Conner?" Rose got my attention. "Do you know the Handmaiden?"

"I know of her," I said. The Handmaiden ran a brothel and stood high among all the madams in town. Famous. I knew of her.

"Dis young lady," Rose bobbed his well-quaffed head toward the tear-stained girl. "She come from da Handmaiden wid a mess."

Well, okay. Maybe she was the mess. I, wisely for an Irishman, remained quiet.

Rose turned toward the well-dressed men lounging on the over delicate furniture. Another bob of the head and those men, except for Sam, stood and walked deeper into the house.

"Dis mess needs cleaning up. I'd like you ta do it. Would you do dat for me, Conner?"

Like I could, like anyone could, say no to Rose Maceo even in those underboss days. I nodded.

"Yes, Mr. Maceo. Of course."

"Good. Dat's good." Rose reached into his pocket to produce his folded wad. He thumbed off some bills. "Here's a yard. Another yard your way when it's done. You take dis girl over to da Handmaiden. She tell you what she needs."

I stepped to take hold of the five one hundred dollar bills. "Yes, sir, Mr. Maceo."

Sam got up, took hold of the girl and walked the two of us out to the porch. The brightest thing out in this darkness was the gleam of his smile. He took hold of my arm as we stepped down to the sidewalk. He let go of the girl.

"Why you, do you think?" Sam asked me as the girl took a couple of steps into the night.

"I haven't been told why me," I answered. In truth, I didn't think it mattered.

"So you know of the Handmaiden?"

I nodded. Her moniker told all about what she did for a living. Or how she had made all her money, if you thought about it.

"What you may not know is that she is a woman of respect and a woman of power," Sam said. "And the lady has a name. It's Dianne."

"Thank you, Mr. Maceo. I appreciate knowing that," I answered and I meant it.

"There. That is why you were chosen. My brother asked for you. He told us you speak correctly and you show respect," Sam said. "Make sure to do so with Miss Dianne. Call her that. Her name is Dianne Starr."

"Yes. Dianne Starr. Miss Dianne."

"That respect is mutual. That is why she sent this young woman to the Beach." Sam gestured to the girl standing in the yard. "She will help, I think."

The Beach. That's what us members of the Beach Gang referred to ourselves. Businesses with place. Not a gang. Not gangsters. Why, how, could the girl help?

"Did you see Schwartz?" Sam said to the night.

I turned to see a hazy grayness slightly lighter than the inky dark. Manny.

"I did," Manny said.

"Get what we need?" Sam asked.

"I did."

Sam turned back to me, eyes shining. "If you need, the Beach can open doors. Use it, if you need. But, be choosy with what you need."

That might have been a word to the wise, I thought. Anyway, Sam turned to return to the house. We were dismissed.

Manny put the woman in the back of his Ford, me in the front, and drove toward my place.

"Here," he said. He shoved a pistol into my stomach. A large, heavy Colt revolver. "From Schwartz. Even if you have your own, use this one."

"Why?" I was always a man of stupid questions.

"It's clean. Rose wants you to have it. But mostly because I said so."

"Gotcha."

"Here're some things about the Handmaiden. Listen." Manny continued. I listened. "She's not a Beach whore. She's independent and she's powerful. The power of knowing many secrets. That ought to be easy enough to figure even for a Paddy."

He grinned. There was no meanness jabbed at me. Just men rousting each other, though I thought better of rousting him back. I grinned.

"Figured," I said.

"A lot of business going back and forth between her and the Beach. A lot of respect back and forth. I don't know what they told you back there, but be sure to kid glove this lady. Polite's the word. Okay?"

"Okay."

"Do what she says. She knows you're coming."

"Me?"

Manny shook his head. "She knows somebody's coming."

"Somebody from the Beach?"

"We help her out, if she asks."

"What's the mess?" I asked.

"Have no idea," Manny said.

I turned to the girl. She sat pushed against the corner of the seat behind me. Her head pressed against the window and she stared, unfocused, into the night.

"Do you know?"

She did not react.

"If she knows, she ain't saying. Not to us anyway," Manny said.

"I'll kid glove her, too."

"Good idea."

No one said anything until we pulled up at my place.

I knuckled my forehead goodbye and stood with the silent girl as

Manny's car puttered off. Porky came up grinning and eyeballing us both.

"Go tell Bobbie Lee to get his stuff," I told him. Bobbie Lee would know what stuff I meant. "Tell him I need his car."

I didn't need to tell him I'd drive. I always drove on Beach business. That was on him, not me. Bobbie Lee insisted on that ever since we were ambushed on a dark Arkansas road, carrying corn squeezings, and he couldn't get to his pistol for having to stop the truck. That might have been the last time the boy ever drove.

Bobbie Lee's Studebaker, with her smooth putter, drifted down the driveway. He didn't look as it stopped, held in place by the dip of the gutter. Those eyes did pop when I popped the suicide door open for the girl. He stared as he slid over to the passenger seat. I hopped in behind the steering wheel.

"This is Bobbie Lee," I said. "Bobbie this, uh, this is somebody."

"Hi, somebody." Bobbie Lee grinned his most appealing grin.

"Livia," she said.

"Hi, Livia."

Livia did not respond.

"Where are we goin'?" Bobbie Lee asked.

"We're going to see the Handmaiden."

"The Handmaiden?" I didn't think Bobbie Lee's eyes could open any wider but he managed it. "Do we get to see any of her whores?"

"I'm one of her whores," Livia said.

I turned to stare. She sat much like she did in Manny's Ford, slumped against the door, head resting against the window. Her legs were slightly parted, the farther knee raised and propped against the door. She noticed my lowered eyes. Not a flicker my way, but she noticed. She did not move. She certainly refused, as most women might, to tug at her skirt. I went back to watching the road.

Bobbie Lee cranked around to face Livia with his whole face in a smile.

"Careful, gangster, you'll pull something," Livia said. "You can't afford me."

Good ol' Bobbie Lee never laid down, never quit. Little as he was, the only stopping him was to kill him. His smile just got bigger, if that was possible.

"Maybe I saved my money," he said.

I glanced back. Livia lifted her head and gave a shadow of a smile.

"Come knock on my door sometime. Maybe I'll let you in."

I chuckled.

"What?" Bobbie Lee asked.

I just shook my head. The vision of those two tangled among a wad of sheets couldn't be unseen. Lightning in a midnight thunderstorm.

Galveston's brothel district started around Post Office Street and Twenty-fifth, and continued up to Twenty-ninth. Most of it on the Town Gang's side of Broadway. We didn't go there. The Handmaiden worked her ladies in a ponderous upscale mansion a little farther up. On K Street and Thirtieth. The ginger-breaded, three-story backed up against a collection of shops that faced the busy artery. Conveniently, for the Handmaiden, each of these had parking areas behind them. A discrete amenity for her top drawer customers.

I parked in front of her house right on K Street. We were not customers needing discretion.

Bobbie Lee jumped out to open Livia's door. She hesitated, terrified.

"Come on, darlin'. We're given a mission," I said.

"I'm not your darling."

"Yep, true. But you are my charge, so you're coming in." I sounded harsher than I wanted to. I guess I was feeling my oats as a gangster.

"You're gonna be fine, Livia." Bobbie Lee winked. "We're your shining knights."

I don't think Livia bought that, but she shot one leg out onto the street and removed herself from my car. Bobbie Lee almost choked and I envied his view.

Any thought of Livia's unladylike exit evaporated when I came around beside her. Purpose, challenge, shone in her eyes. Dared to say something, I stayed silent. She had some fight left in her. A good thing. Why would I think that?

We found the Handmaiden standing in the footpath slashing her back garden in half. A small woman whose dark clothing glittered in the glare of bare-bulb lights strung above the head high shrubbery. Her "close" friend, Mary stood, as if at attention, next to her. I knew her, and her reputation, as Contrary Mary.

The two women nodded to each other at our arrival. They were a mismatched pair. Contrary Mary, tall, handsome, and with her boyish hair bob, wore a man's tuxedo and a bitter frown. Strange to know, Mary had a reputation as a knife fighter. No one wanted to be cut by Contrary Mary. The Handmaiden, Miss Dianne, maybe reached five three or four in her strapped heels. Wispy blonde curls moved, touched by the breeze. Her eyes were as pale a blue as Bobbie Lee's. A nice-sized strawberry birthmark spread across the right cheek of her innocently attractive face, though I doubted there was much that was innocent about the Handmaiden. She wore a clinging, black dress, short enough to show knees and rich with sequins that sparkled.

Miss Dianne looked at us with open curiosity.

"Ollie send you?" she asked, as if doubting we were up for the job.

"Mr. Maceo, ma'am."

"Sam?"

"Rose, ma'am."

"Should've known. And I'm Dianne Starr, or Dianne. Not Ma'am."

"Sorry, ma'am. I mean, sorry Miss Dianne."

The woman winked at Mary. "Where're you from, cowboy? East Texas somewhere?"

"A little nothing town called Alto. Outside of it, really."

"I know that town. I'm a Longview girl." She smiled.

I smiled back as I was supposed to. "Been there a couple of times."

"So why did Rose say he was sending you over to the Handmaiden's whorehouse?"

That was blunt enough. "Said I was to help clean up a mess."

She paused then seemed to notice the girl.

"Are you all right, Livia?"

"I am." A quiet reply. An uncomfortable one.

"Then go on in to the front parlor. I'll be there soon."

I didn't turn to see Livia's reaction, if there was one. I listened to her walk away.

"So, cowboy, what 'cha do before you came down to the island? Truth now?"

"Bootlegging," I truthed. She raised an eyebrow. "Ran corn liquor up to Louisiana and Arkansas."

"Why did you come down here?"

"Had to lam."

"Of course." She paused again. "I guess you'll do. Let's go see my mess."

Miss Dianne's mess was murder.

Pedro "Peter" Godines turned out to be the name of the stiff. In a pool of his own blood, he laid piled like dirty laundry on the flagstone walkway. The second murdered body I'd seen. Didn't care to see another one.

Bobbie Lee let out a low whistle. "Damn. Maybe we could borrow a tarpaulin, or a blanket, or something."

"Now why on earth would you want that?" the Handmaiden, Miss Dianne, asked.

Once again my eyes drifted down to her hands. Blood, heat, stirred within me.

"Well, that's the mess, right? What do you want us to do with the body? Take it to the Gulf?" Bobbie Lee asked.

"You will not," Miss Diane harrumphed. "Peter was a good enough man. Regular. Didn't rough anyone up. Got Ralph, Doctor

Kennedy, coming. He'll get Peter down to the funeral home. Get him tended to proper. Anyway, that's not my mess."

"Sorry ma'am. I am," Bobbie Lee quailed. I'd stressed doing the Handmaiden right on the drive up.

"Well, bless your heart, youngster," she said. When my old aunts used that term it generally meant, 'die and go to hell.' She nodded to Mary. "Handle things. Me and the boys'll go in."

The woman's office, lair more like, glowed in oiled walnut. Solid walnut desk and leather chair. Walnut shelves, cabinets, and wax-shiny walls. Gas lamps of black iron, one high center of each wall, beat back the dim. Below the lamp, facing the opulent desk, hung an antique map of the world, original and real.

Opposite the entry was an open door. I could see a fancy loveseat backed against a whitewashed wall. Lit up like a stage prop.

Miss Dianne, the Handmaiden, noticed my gaze. She smiled. The woman was quite fetching.

"You know why I'm famous. What I'm famous for," she said. The mischief in her eyes, decorated by that birthmark on her cheek, caused her to look younger than I figured her. Early thirties, maybe. Late twenties. Miss Dianne earned her fame some years before I stepped onto the Island.

"Yes." I nodded.

"Go ahead, have your peek. What I do is sort of a peep show anyway."

I took her up on it, with Bobbie Lee close on my heels.

The room, larger than I thought, stretched back into a dark recess. All the other walls were flat black. Across from the loveseat, in the dark, was a barely seen, over-stuffed couch and foot stool.

"Pretty quiet these days," she continued. "And usually empty."

"Too busy now?" Bobbie Lee asked, looking in.

Miss Diane gave a throaty chuckle. "Some old customers that I like special. A few others. Let's say I hand pick them."

You could probably hear Bobbie Lee swallow all the way to Houston. I bit back a snigger. Miss Dianne closed the door.

She came around to sit behind her desk. With a gesture, she motioned us into our own chairs.

"So, the cleanup of my mess. I want the bastard that did this. That's what I'm sending you out to do."

"Yessum." The answer automatic. This dumb Paddy was not used to that kind of language out of a lady's mouth.

Miss Dianne laughed. "You know something about chasing down murderers, do you, Conner?"

I didn't, and wisely kept my flushed face silent.

"Thought not."

"Well, ma'am," Bobbie Lee intruded. "Them that get dead up home usually get that way 'cause somebody gets somethin' out of it."

"Know anybody that'd get something out of seeing him killed?"

Bobbie Lee did not.

"Miss Dianne," I started. "I may be ignorant of all this, but it seems to me it's a hunt. I hunt. The hardest things to hunt up home are chicken-killing coyotes and garbage-thieving coons. You find the trail and chase 'em down. So I figure we go looking for a trail."

"Neither of those critters killed Peter, I don't think," she said. To take my mind off the hand resting on the Handmaiden's desk, I studied the birth mark staining her cheek.

"Both come to feed where they shouldn't. I'll go find who feeds off this man's death." I tried to sound confident. Somehow I could not be letting Rose Maceo down. That meant I'd have to be helping out here.

"Sounds Like you know something about critters. You'll need to learn about Peter."

"Yes, Miss Dianne." There was nothing else to say.

"And, children, you might want to consider that you could get hunted back. Folks take a dim view of being hunted."

I figured she had the right of that.

"So," she went on. "I want you to take Livia with you."

"What?" I said. If I was going to be hunted, I didn't figure Livia should be anywhere close to me.

"I don't think Livia saw anything. She says she didn't." Dianne said. "But whoever did this may have caught sight of her. He might want to fix that loose end. You won't mind that will you?"

"You think she'll be safe around me?"

"Don't take her hunting with you. But I suspect she'll not be real safe staying here."

I shrugged. "If you think it's best."

"Livia's not white. At least, not all white." The Handmaiden turned her hand palm up. "That might bother some Texans."

"I'm not one of those kind of Texans."

"Me neither," Bobbie Lee said brightly.

"You treat that girl nice," the Handmaiden warned. "She's been through it tonight."

We both nodded.

A BROWN SUIT

Bobbie Lee and I kid-gloved Livia all the way back to my place. Her silence persisted and I didn't push her. I did put a set of clean sheets in her hand and closed the bedroom door on her. Bobbie Lee went on home. I tried to sleep on my sorry excuse for a couch.

Livia, a peek of black hair and bare knee, did not move when I eased into the room for some clean clothes. Bobbie Lee showed up for coffee around six. With dire warnings to be a gentleman, I left him tending Livia and headed to the Blue Plate for some eggs.

By seven, I was wandering the Handmaiden's back garden. I guessed the back gate of a whorehouse is rarely locked.

A throaty, liquid cough, the cough of an old ex-boxer that spent too many hours nursing cigars, reminded me that it was too early to be here. And a notice that I was being watched. Ignoring him, I continued nosing around.

The cello-squeaking sound of a screen door spring announced a new arrival. I turned at the bang of the door. Contrary Mary stepped down the stairs wearing nothing but a farmer's overalls.

Nothing but a farmer's overalls and a curious frown. Most alluring.

Most disconcerting.

"Good morning, Miss Mary." I tipped my fedora.

"Drop the Miss. I'm Miss to nobody. It's Conner, right?"

"Yessum."

"Kinda early for a Paddy to be out and about. What you doing?"

Mary hooked thumbs under the bib of those overalls and important parts seemed to want to fall out of those things.

"Uh, well, I guess it is. I guess."

Mary's handsome rather than pretty face showed amusement at my stammer.

"Miss Dianne and I talked about this being a sort of hunt," I added. "So I thought I might find a track or two."

"Did you?"

"Not really. Your ladies seem to spend a lot of time walking the maze."

"Yeah, they do. At least when there's more of them than there are customers."

"Whoever came for Mr. Godines plowed up everything over there." I pointed to where I'd seen the body. "I didn't find any sign of anyone hiding in wait."

"What kind of sign would that be?" Mary asked.

"I don't know. A flattened down place among your shrubbery made by somebody hiding. A pile of cigarette butts all stepped on. Stuff like that."

"Did you see any of that?"

"No. Whoever killed him must have walked right up to him and did the deed. Was he shot? Cut? Do you know?"

"Haven't heard."

Geez, that woman had nice skin. And a lot of it seemed to be spilling out of those overalls. Pretty feet, too, as she stood barefooted on the path.

"I guess I gotta find another kind of trail," I said. "Just who is our dead man? Do you know that?"

"Peter Godines, though I suspect he's really Pedro Godines, is some mucky-muck lawyer for Seaways Shipping Company," Contrary Mary, half in and half out of her overalls, said.

"Shipping?"

"No. Warehousing and transport. Taking things from the ships to the mainland. They're pretty big up town, as far as I know. He's married."

"A married man?" I asked, all wide-eyed.

Mary chuckled. A sultry chuckle from down in her throat. "Most men that show up at our door are married. Kind of tells you something about wives, huh?"

That was a puzzle. I sure didn't know what it told about wives. If Mary knew what it was, she wasn't telling. We kind of stood there quiet for a moment.

"Is the man's company a Town Gang concern?"

"Wouldn't know. Probably not," Mary returned. "You gangsters are small time really. Compared to big business, you guys are chump change."

"So maybe this is something more. Something besides a murder in a..." I didn't finish the thought. Mary did, though.

"Murder in a whorehouse? Wouldn't know. Probably not. Still want to get a hold of whoever did this. You find him. Bring him to me," Contrary Mary said. She turned to walk back, knowing exactly the effect she was having on me. "See you soon."

I took a last look at her nice shoulders and left to find what I could find.

How do I find a murderer? I sure didn't know back then. There were no footprints or cigarette butts to follow. No dropped gun. No witnesses speaking up. In fact, I didn't know squat except that Mr. Peter Godines got found in a puddle of blood in a whorehouse garden. I figured the best thing to do was to go find him. That meant a short drive over to the Stennis and Sons Funeral Parlor. That's where, in Galveston, all the murdered folks started, until families found something else to do with them.

Coming from the Beach opened that door as well. Almost wish

it hadn't. The somber, pale, and well-starched attendant escorted me to the preparation room. The place looked more like the kitchen of a restaurant than what I expected. Mr. Godines lay on a metal table covered with a sheet. Three large porcelain sinks lined a wall. A long black water hose snaked from one of the sinks across the floor to the table to rest next to a big galvanized tank on wheels. A couple of metal cabinets sat against another wall. Dr. Kennedy and the funeral parlor's ghoul stood at the table considering Mr. Godines.

Often enough the undertakers in town did the duties of coroners. At least unofficially. I guess this stiff earned the direct attention of the good doctor. Word had it that among his other services was a leather case full of hypodermic needles holding what you needed when you needed it. And he was the man to see for girls in trouble that needed their trouble removed. Hence, his relationship to Dianne "the Handmaiden" Starr.

Kennedy fixed a suspicious eye on me.

"So? What the hell are you doing here?" he asked in a throaty baritone.

"I'm Miss Starr's cleanup crew." I tried brazen.

"How'd you get to be that?"

A puzzle worth thinking about. The answer I needed to give was anyway. "I got sent down from the Beach."

"Well, ain't that a candy-coated delight. Ol' Ollie got his nose in the shit. Again."

I figured it best not to reply to that. Mr. Quinn wasn't getting anything but respect out of me.

"What did Stern want?" Kennedy continued.

"Stern?"

"Yeah, Stern. German for Star. That's her real name."

"My best guess is that she wants whoever killed this man," I said.

Kennedy considered a moment, then rolled his eyes. "I don't know who the hell killed him."

"Did he get shot?" I asked.

Kennedy's stare got harder, if that was possible. "Come over here, boy. Get your nose in it."

The ghoul folded down the sheet from Godines' head and stepped back.

Getting close to dead people has never been one of my favorite things but I took tentative steps over to the table. Kennedy pointed a middle finger to the man's neck.

"That look like a bullet hole?"

Half lost in a dark blue, bruised looking neck was a small, black hole. I shook my head. "No."

"Doesn't to me either."

"How does something like that kill a person?"

"Permanently," Kennedy answered.

I think he expected me to laugh at the joke. I did not laugh.

"All right. Unfortunately for Mr. Godines, this little poke got done with some real muscle. It got jammed in here." Kennedy pointed again at the little black hole. I managed to keep from gagging. "Then on through the back of his larynx, his voice box. That's probably why no one heard any yelling. And on its way right into the man's jugular. Bled right out, he did."

"I didn't see all that much blood out there in the garden," I said.

"Over to the Handmaiden's house, were you?" Kennedy sounded a bit smirky.

I did not respond.

"Godines did most of his bleeding on the inside. Heart drove all that blood down into his chest and belly. That's why he looks so bloated fat." Kennedy prodded the swollen belly with a finger.

"Knife? Splinter? What did that?" I asked.

Kennedy stared down at the body a moment. "Best guess? Ice pick. Some sort of marlinspike, maybe?"

"What's a marlinspike?"

"Something sailors use to do their rope work. Ran across some injuries from them. Some kind of brawl down at the shrimper docks a couple of years ago."

I gave that a bit of thought. For no reason I could name, I figured spikes and picks are things of fury. Seemed like there would be a bunch of holes poked into poor Mr. Godines.

"Do you know the man?" I asked.

"I knew of him."

"Prominent?"

"A bit. I guess. He runs with the top drawer bunch. At least some of them."

"Some?"

"The Moody family don't like him much. Some of the business owners out at the wharf. The dock workers, too."

"Why the Moodys?" I asked. The Moody family stood among the town fathers, had hands in most of the deep pockets, and had more money than God, as far as I knew.

"Some of those companies Moody does that thing for, that insurance thing, compete with his company. I don't know much about it."

"The dock workers?"

"Now that's an angry bunch. Some of them anyway. I hear that he got the Negro stevedores to get together. Promised to work for less than the white ones, then got his company to hire a bunch of them. That made a pile of money for Seaways Shipping and caused the competition to lower wages for all dock workers."

"That makes for a lot of enemies."

Kennedy nodded.

"I wonder if that's all of them." I said to myself.

"Have you spoken to Godines' wife?"

"No."

"I think she might be over in the chapel. She and her maid brought over a suit."

"Brown." The mortician disapproved of the choice of colors.

I had an idea, finding the two women in the chapel, that Mrs. Godines and her Negro maid had attended funerals before. They were dressed for one. The widow's black cloche hung low across her brow, sporting a brooch of onyx surrounded by diamonds, with a brush spray clinging close to her skull. She had affixed a black, gossamer veil spilling over her face and shoulders. The veil did not hide a black jacket and a black skirt. Black lace decorated the hems of sleeves and skirt. A severe frown chiseled the woman's face as she sat in the front pew staring at the floor.

Her companion turned to face me as I entered. A wide-brimmed hat, swooping low, did not blunt angry eyes. She also had a long veil draped over her widow-black dress, long-sleeved with a gather of belted cloth low on her hips. Her hand held a beaded clutch purse.

"May I help you, sir?" the maid said as I approached. Her eyes gave me the once over, dingy suit, scuffed shoes, weathered hat, and all.

"I hope to speak to Mrs. Godines, if she's able," I said.

"You do not remove your hat in the presence of a lady and in a holy place?" the woman said in a voice of pure vinegar.

I cringed and jerked the fedora off my head, feeling my skewed hair.

"May I?" I asked and took a step.

"You certainly may not. You dare? My mistress mourns."

The withering stare and Dallas drawl locked into my soul and remains vivid down to this day. I was determined, however.

"Only a moment, I swear," I said over the maid's shoulder to the widow.

"It's all right, Dora," Mrs. Godines said.

"This ain't no regular fellah. Looks like plain riff-raff to me. Street trash."

"Forgive my companion. She is very protective of those she cares for." Mrs. Godines straightened in the pew, but didn't turn toward me.

I walked gingerly around the women. All my tough, probing questions fled me. Being near a new widow, I guess. I sat but not too close to her.

"Are you riff-raff, sir?" Mrs. Godines asked. She did not look at me.

I glanced at her a second, then decided to give her the right answer. "Yes, ma'am. Riff-raff."

She turned to me then. A handsome woman. Mid-thirties. Dark piercing eyes. Roman nose and strong jaw.

"Let me take this fool up by the ear and march him right outta here," Dora said.

"Do I know you, sir?" Mrs. Godines ignored the maid. "Do you know my – did you know my husband?"

"No, ma'am."

"Then why are you here?"

Why was I here? I came to find out who the man's enemies were. Maybe who killed him. But that had to do with Dr. Kennedy, and maybe with the stiff.

For the first time, Mrs. Godines looked at me. Her dark eyes stared into mine. I didn't see a lot of mourning in them. Not much helplessness either. Well, her husband had been found dead in the whorehouse garden. I guessed I wouldn't mourn much myself.

"No reason, ma'am. Just that I hope that better days come to you soon," I managed.

I took my hat in my hand and stood. Mrs. Godines' companion appeared at my side. Up close, Dora had to be two inches taller than me and quite fearsome.

"I'll see you out of here, trash." She took a grip on my arm and half dragged me all the way to the entry. "I don't expect to see you again."

Dora turned on her heel. I watched as the woman marched back into the shadow.

"My Momma? I don't know," Bobbie Lee said. His eyes drifted to the wall over my head and filled with sadness. "The only thing I remember of her is her describing that little cottage she always wanted. My poor Pa never scraped up enough money to buy it for her. Funny thing, I can see that cottage a lot more clear than I can see my Momma's face."

Papa and I exchanged a glance, not really knowing that kind of thought could come out of the boy.

"What about yours, Papa?" Bobbie Lee asked.

Papa growled and turned back to sort the nickels from the quarters.

I laughed. "Papa and a mother? Ha, he leaped, fully formed, from some seed pod just as we see him."

"Here. Work while you blather." Papa shoved a pile of quarters at me. "Anyway, what of that Irish quiff that calls herself your mother?"

"Why, do you mean that sparkling glow of Celtic beauty and virtue, that angel of East Texas warmth and nurture?"

"Okay, I guess that depends on who's looking when," Papa said with an evil grin.

"Don't know. Been years," I said, ready enough to talk of something else. "What were we saying anyway?"

"We were talking about how you useless boys got down to the Island so that I got stuck with you." Papa shoved more quarters at me.

"No we weren't," Bobbie Lee put in. "I asked you if you knew how the Handmaiden got to be who she got to be."

"Yeah, Papa, that's the story I want to hear."

"Me too." Livia came in from the kitchen carrying beers.

Canadian bottled beers that Papa brought with him. Their corks were latched down with wire. Livia levered the wires and prized out the corks and passed them around.

"This is a nice treat, Papa. Thanks." I took a sip.

"Well, thank the girl there." He pointed his bottle at Livia. "Because of her, this is my last night bossin' the two of you around. Least for a while."

"Sorry, Mr. Regelo," Livia said.

"Pshaw. Look at 'em. Two less worthless Paddies. No great loss." Papa lowered his eyes and pursed his lips, like he did when he picked at us.

"Yeah, yeah, we'll not miss you, too. Now tell us about the Handmaiden," Bobbie Lee prompted.

"You can thank Ollie Quinn for that."

"Ollie Quinn?"

"Your boss. His boss." Papa nodded first at Bobbie Lee then at me. "My boss. Everybody's boss."

Well, he was boss of the Beach Gang.

"Ahh, give me my youth back." Papa drifted into some private reverie. Then he went on. "Had my own crew then. Nobody between me and Ollie. Took skim off every boat going or coming. Course, we ended up with Prohibition. Made more money when those fools made us go dry."

"You miss it?" Livia asked.

"No, girl, I don't. I'm just too damn old."

"What's old about you, handsome?" Livia cooed.

Papa smiled, clearly pleased, but he shook his head. He shot me a look. "Good luck, friend. I think you're gonna need it."

"Thank Ollie for what?" Bobbie Lee steered Papa back to the truly important conversation.

"Mr. Quinn. Remember that, boy," Papa said.

"Mr. Quinn, then."

"According to Ollie, Dianne showed up here about ten years back. With Contrary Mary. Seems wherever they were from didn't cotton to... to, you know, girls like them."

"True. I know something about that end of the world," I said. "Or, any end of the world, far as I know."

Papa started stacking nickels in towers of ten. "Ollie told me they hustled on the street, at first. Kinda like you, Conner."

I nodded at that. Bobbie Lee and I swept and mopped a bunch of stores. Washed some cars. That kind of stuff. Some days we weren't even hungry.

"Didn't always go well for 'em. But folks learned to respect Mary's knife. Not like Mary, Dianne didn't hold much against men. Ollie told me she started fiddling..." Papa paused.

Livia shrugged. "Gave 'em a tug, did she? Don't worry, Papa, I know how she... well, what she did to earn her way."

"A dollar a time. So Ollie told me," Papa went on. "Got popular. Some of the house owners and pimps complained at the loss of income. At least, they did until Contrary Mary got contrary with 'em."

"I bet she did," Livia said, admiration plain on her face.

"Finally, ol' Fat Phil. Any of you know that name?" Papa waited until we all shook our heads. "He wasn't fat. He was a stick. But he owned a couple of bakeries. Made everybody else fat..."

"The Handmaiden, man," Bobbie Lee interrupted. "Anyway, do you know how she even knew about that talent of hers?"

"I know that," Livia said. "The girls say that she walked in and caught her uncle strumming his fiddle. A couple of times, apparently. She got curious. Asked him about it. The story goes that he taught her how. She started helping out. That's what they say anyway."

"Jesus," Bobbie Lee sighed.

Papa went on as if he didn't even hear Livia. "Ol' Fat Phil wasn't no fool. Not him. He up and bought that whorehouse closest to the Gulf. Started tapping the casinos along there. Well, Dianne had been going out there. Baiting the fishermen, if you know what I mean."

This time Livia groaned.

"Anyway, Ol' Phil figured she could give him a hand, so to speak." Papa dropped his eyes and pursed his lips, pleased with his string of puns.

We all groaned.

"Dianne got herself a room in Fat Phil's. Got popular. Made a deal with Phil. He was happy. Charged a full two dollars, just like a full treatment with any of the girls. So he'd get his cut. Even got Contrary Mary's help keeping the marks in line. That broad was tougher than any bouncer he had. That's where Ollie caught ear of 'em."

"Didn't know Mr. Quinn went to such places," Bobbie Lee put in.

"He doesn't. Why would he need to? Women drop on him like rain on dirt."

"Then, how...?" I started.

"Trouble. Some soldiers getting too drunk. Getting out of hand. Ollie took a bunch of us over there before it got spread out to the casinos. We ran down by his place. It was handled before we got there."

"Contrary Mary?"

"You bet. We hung around a bit. Just in case. And Ollie heard about the new talent. The Handmaiden. Before the night was done, Ollie gave her the idea that made her the success she is today," Papa said.

"He told her to get a girl not busy to pose. Naked. While she fiddled with her mark," said Livia.

"For a dollar extra," Papa added.

That brought work to a stop as Bobbie Lee and I pondered Mr. Quinn's genius.

Papa winked at Livia. "Boys, huh?"

"Boys and men, Papa. Ya'll are strange. All of ya'll." Livia gave each of us a disapproving once-over and headed to the kitchen.

Us boys and men exchanged glances, half mischief, half embarrassment. We probably were strange. At least to most women.

"Yeah, maybe," Bobbie Lee said. "But they give us lots of fun stuff to be strange about."

True enough.

"So, Conner, how was it you two got down to the Island. Smackover, wasn't it?"

Yeah. Smackover. Smackover, Arkansas. Five hundred oil wells growing like a fungus in the middle of muddy, forested hills. Five hundred oil wells, forty saloons, and as many whorehouses. Myself, Bobbie Lee, and a crew of four other bootleggers took up residence in a widow's barn just out of town. From there, We supplied the roughnecks with a river of moonshine.

"You were there, right?" Papa went on. "At least until the citizens remembered their religion. Them and the Klan. We heard about the riot way down here. Run the bootleggers, saloon keepers, and whores clear out of town, huh?"

"Got warned out, actually," Bobbie Lee said.

Papa raised bushy, curious eyebrows.

"We had a sheriff in our pocket. Gave us a heads up." I shrugged.

"And you come all the way down here?"

"When we got back we found our boss doing a stretch in Angola. Got caught on the Louisiana border."

"Things had dried up. Galveston seemed promising. So here we are," Bobbie Lee added.

"Missed the tar and feathers then?" Papa asked.

"And the buckshot and the whip." I nodded.

CLINCKSCALES

A BRIGHT, MIDDAY SUN SHIMMERED THE HOMES AND SHOPS along Broadway. A sultry breeze shaved off some of the heat. The outbound electric trolley clattered by. A second or two later an inbound one did the same. They rang bells at each other. An ice truck ground its gears as it tried to gain speed on its way to town. Probably toward the fisherman's wharf. Other traffic sputtered or growled up and down the way.

I was at a loss. What did I know? Dead man. Whorehouse. Dry-eyed widow. An indifferent doctor. What was I doing? I shook my head. Surely the Galveston cops would stir up the murderer. Long before I had a chance to even come close. On second thought, maybe not. The city cops were good enough at what they did despite spending time in the pockets of a slew of businessmen and a fist full of gangs. I chuckled. Gangs busy plying their trades in service to a sin-hungry bunch of citizens and visitors. I was sure they were looking hard. But they'd be looking for muggers, cut-purses, or roaming crazy people. Something in my gut nagged me into thinking there was something else to it.

I bet that Rose Maceo thought so as well. Why else would he send me out to the Handmaiden?

A gust of wind pressed against my clothes. It caused me to feel the wad of hundreds jammed deep into my pocket. I knew that was one reason why I was doing it.

I also knew that Peter Godines was a lawyer. Back then, I figured that lawyers ran in packs. The only pack wolf the bottom feeders of the Beach gang knew was the Rabid Scotsman, Luthias Clinkscales. Called the Rabid Scotsman for his snarl of a voice, an icy stare, and a storm of red-gold hair on face and head. Atty. Clinkscales showed up at the jail and the courthouse whenever we got pinched. We were at the bottom of the pile. Ollie Quinn, the Maceo brothers, the others on the top of the pile, all had their own.

I found the lawyer at the Galveston Country Club off 61st Street and Avenue S. Specifically, in the dressing room of its golf course. His home away from home. He sat on a bench knifing mud and grit from a pair of hard-used golfing shoes. I stood before him as he ignored me. A lot of folks seemed hell bent on ignoring me that day.

"Who screwed up this time?" Clinkscales said without looking up from his chore. He was a big, well-fed man, hunched over in his undershirt and plaid knickerbockers. The red hair flamed over his back, arms and chest. A cloud of whiskey surrounded him.

"No one, sir. None that I know of," I answered.

"Then," he looked up at me with fierce eyes. "Speak to me, kid."

"I come from the Beach." I figured it would help if I played that card first.

"So?" Clinkscales rumbled.

"Do you know Peter Godines? You being a lawyer and all."

"I know he's dead." Clinkscales sat up a bit and laid his knife hand on his knee. He sighed. "Not a personal friend, but I knew him when I saw him. We shook hands a time or two."

"Who'd be his enemies?" I asked, trying to find a place to start. "The Moodys maybe?"

Clinkscales laughed. "The Moodys. Now that'd be enemies to have, by God."

The Moodys, like the Sealys and the Kempners, were the big money on the Island. Big money for anywhere in the world, as far as I could figure.

"Maybe. Maybe a few years ago. Now days, old man Moody spends all of his time playing with cotton and oil. He is one son-of-a-bitch, like his daddy, but he's really given up fighting over control of the wharf. Anyway, I doubt he even knows Godines exists. Not the same circles at all."

"Sealys? Kempners?"

Another half-swallowed laugh.

"Same side, actually," he continued. "That bunch control the wharves. And, the wharves are a hobby of our Pedro Godines. Or the colored stevedores are anyway, when he's not overseeing Seaways transportation contracts."

"Stevedores as a hobby?"

"Sure. He sort of does for them like I do for you Beach toughs."

"So, he's popular, huh?"

Clinkscales shrugged noncommittedly. "There may be an angle there."

"What angle?"

"The ol' boy had a reputation for sniffing around those dock workers' sisters. Couldn't keep his hands off 'em is what I hear."

"Mr. Godines is turning out to be a real busy man," I said. "Especially with negro women."

"Yep. Gotta admire the man." Clinkscales started in on the muddy golf shoes again. "You know, he's got one he keeps over in some hovel. Heard she's a right pretty thing. She might know something."

"How could I go about finding her?"

"Don't know. Ask some of those dock workers." Clinkscales thumbed a cleat on one of his shoes. "And buy yourself a new suit."

I told him I would do both. However, neither happened that day.

Two big tankers were tied off, and every man I could see was offloading crates of produce at a dead run. Ignoring me completely. Again.

I drove home, stopping to get a few groceries and the afternoon paper, and skipping the men's stores.

No one noticed me pushing the door open with a foot. Livia and Bobbie Lee danced frantically to the scratchy, chaotic jazz being played on the Victrola. Bobbie Lee's arms flayed and legs kicked and stomped as he tried to match her moves. Livia? Livia was lost in the music and in the moment.

Manny Dents slouched on my couch with a pleasant enough smile on his mug. His eyes busied themselves watching Livia's flashing gams. I'd be smiling too. She had a pair. Manny interrupted his reverie to glance and nod as I walked by. He followed me into the kitchen.

"How'd it go?" Manny rummaged through the paper sacks. I shrugged. "Nothing?"

"Nothing much," I said. "I went to see Clinkscales earlier."

"Clinkscales? Why him?"

"Godines was a lawyer. Clinkscales is the only lawyer I know. Maybe they were friends."

"Were they?" Manny pulled out the beer and grabbed one for himself.

"No," I answered. "Knew each other in passing. The old goat gave me a couple of ideas, though. Said Godines does – did — lawyering for all the colored workmen out on the wharves. Maybe he was in on the fight between the Sealys and the Moodys a while back. He also likes to play hands with the colored girls."

Manny grinned. "That can be fun."

I nodded. It could be. "I also went to the funeral parlor. Saw old Dr. Kennedy."

"Doctor Fix It."

"I like that. Doctor Fix It," I said. "Anyway, he had me thinking. Do you know anybody in town that likes using an ice pick?"

That put puzzle on Manny's face. "No, I don't. Not right off hand."

"How about a marlinspike?"

"What's a marlinspike?"

"It's like an icepick for a shrimper."

"A shrimper," Manny laughed. "I wouldn't put anything past one of those boys."

"I plan on going down to their docks in a day or two."

"Take help. Those bastards are crazy."

"Wanta come?"

"I'm doing the up-and-down this week," he said. The up-and-down meant Manny and his crew toured the joints looking for trouble from the marks. Squashing any they found. Sort of like cops for the Beach gang's properties. "Maybe another time."

I laughed but with no humor. That was crap duty and a way to get out of helping me. Still, better him than me. Rousting drunks and soldiers was not a fun job. "I'll be careful."

"That beer for anyone?" Bobbie Lee popped through the doorway, Livia right behind. Jazz still squeaked from the Victrola.

I shoved two of them into Bobbie Lee's hands and put the rest in the ice box.

"New clothes?" I asked Livia. She wore a flouncy beige dress belted low on her hips.

"No. Manny brought me some things. Dianne sent them along. Wanta dance?"

"I'm sorry. I don't dance," I said and rued the disappointment that erased her smile. "Saved your feet some sore toes, though."

"Let's go out then. I'm bored." Livia's expectant grin returned.

I looked at Bobbie Lee, hoping to see good reasons to stay put. He only shrugged.

"I don't know. Where did you want to go?"

"Joyland."

"It may not be safe."

"If there's anyone looking for me at all, they'll be looking at Dianne's house."

I looked to Manny next.

"Well, thinking of it," he said. "I don't ever remember seeing any wise guys at Joyland."

"You were there," I said, "You're one of those guys."

"Well, I was the only one."

I gave up. "Joyland."

JOYLAND

Joyland. Galveston's great cathedral to the gods of indulgence. Noise and glitter. Lights and color. And right across Seawall Blvd. from the Gulf.

I found a spot for the Studebaker a couple of blocks down 20th Street. The breeze was gentle as dusk approached. The three of us rounded onto Seawall to stroll alongside Joyland's Garden of Tokyo, touted as the world's largest outdoor dancehall. Some local bunch pounded out jazz for a handful of couples already glowing from the cloud of lightbulbs strung from poles overhead.

I guessed that the Garden's arches and partially red-tiled roof looked Japanese enough with the upturned ends tacked on. Paper lanterns muted the light beneath the pavilion where the band played and tables offered patrons rest and refreshments.

"Jesus, I love Joyland," Livia breathed, wide eyes filling with sights as we entered the Park proper.

Above us, the airplane swing spun wild circles at the top of its beamed tower. On our left the life-sized wooden horses of The Great American Racing Derby clattered and squealed down its huge track. That was supposed to be the world's largest merry-go-round.

It was big enough to make a believer out of me. Its sign stated that medical personnel were available for anyone overcome by the dizzying speed. Between us and the Mountain Speedway rollercoaster sprawled the midway, crowded with concessions, various arcades, a peep show tent, and even a freak show. The freak show was new.

Livia's warm hand drug me to a booth and her hungry eyes pled. I plopped down a dime and a leering old man gave her a candy apple. Bobbie Lee appeared, face covered in butter, holding corn-on-the-cob on a stick. I just shook my head.

We strolled and I was charmed watching Livia drink in all the sights.

"You're taking me there." She nodded at the peepshow as we passed it. "Not now but before we go home."

I was astonished as much by the girl calling my walkup home as by her wanting to enter such a place.

Livia tossed the half-eaten apple. "Rollercoaster first."

Every ride. Didn't miss one. I was glad I skipped the food vendors.

Livia attacked each ride with all the joy of a born warrior. Not the squeals of a little girl but laughter, pure and unfettered. Watching her was sheer delight. No yesterday, no tomorrow, Livia was right now. Or, so I thought. At first.

On the Ferris wheel, she leaned forward, lips parted, death grip on the handle bar. I leaned back enjoying her being close. Enjoying the peek of hose tops embracing rounded thighs. Enjoying knees that never seemed to touch each other.

More laughter riding the rollercoaster. Another hard grasp on the bar. But the grip did not keep her from being thrown against me at each twist and turn. Leg, hip, and shoulder pressed me.

Livia was pure murder on the Great American Racing Derby. She broke hearts, even mine, when she hiked up her skirt, threw a foot into the stirrup, and slung herself astraddle the full-sized wooden horse.

She won that race by two links despite how hard us jockeys fought to catch up to her. I suspected the ride boss.

Confirmed when we left his over-sized tent.

"Your next ride's free, you bring that girl," he leered.

I shot him a look but I couldn't wipe off his smirk.

Livia laid that soft warm hand on mine and drug me to the Penny Arcade.

Penny? It cost two bits to get in. I was real hesitant. The Arcade was not a place for females. Livia sensed my hesitation. She just pulled harder.

Bobbie Lee, chin shiny and another corn cob in hand, waited for us. I raised an eyebrow at him.

He shrugged. "She said ya'll were coming here. I wanna go too."

"You can come," Livia said.

"I don't know. Looks like you be liking my friend, Conner Miles, more than me." He pouted his lower lip.

Livia laughed that crystalline laugh of hers. "I like you too, Bobbie Lee."

She patted his arm and drew out his smile.

"Do you think they'll let you in?" Bobbie Lee asked.

"Take a guess," Livia grinned.

"Yeah. I suppose Jesus himself would let you go in."

Livia laughed as she stepped up to the counter. Bobbie Lee and I were not the only pairs of eyes that watched her.

Painted up like a circus tent, the wooden structure was quite substantial. The inside resembled a pre-prohibition bar. Instead of tables, rows of Kinetoscopes lined either side. And a small stage on the far end.

We entered, a sign promising thrills and chills on "Modern Edison Kinetoscopes and Kinetographs" and telling us that "The Beautiful Princess Rani of the Grand Court of Deli" would do the "Dance of the Seven Veils" at 10 p.m. "Men Only."

"We'll skip the dance," Livia said, then laughed at Bobbie Lee's disappointed groan. "I know Princess Rani. She's no more a princess than me. When she's not entertaining Negro businessmen down on Post Office, she's doing the hoochie coochie over at Jasper's Night Club."

That particular area of Galveston's red light district catered to the wants and needs of the colored folks. A raucous good time to one and all, or so I'd been told. By-and-large, things were fairly peaceful between the races in town, but segregation was the rule.

We, or at least Livia and Bobbie Lee, ignored the stares of the all-male clientele. I was a bit disappointed at most of the Kinetoscope's selections. We dropped our pennies in the slots and turned the cranks. A white horse trotted in slow motion. Two steaming trains collided. The famous, mustached cowboy drew his six-shooter, pointed it at me, and pulled the trigger. I did like the fan dancer artfully hiding her best parts with a storm of ostrich plumes. Even better, the meaty, nude ballerina treating everyone to all her mounds and canyons.

Livia straightened up after cranking through her Kinetoscope peep of the naked dancer.

"I wonder how much she got paid to do that?" she asked.

"More than she thought, I bet. But less than she deserved."

She smiled. "You enjoyed that, did you?"

"Yes, ma'am."

"Always the honest Paddy."

I shrugged. Livia gazed at me with a peculiar expression.

"What?" I asked.

"Wondering. I'm trying to see what's wrong with you."

"I'm sorry?"

"What's not right with the way you look."

Surprised and a bit insulted was the way I looked.

"Don't take it wrong. You're a good looking enough man. Tall. Dark hair. Not fat. Broad shoulders. Good chin."

"But?"

"I know," she said after an uncomfortable pause. "You don't have any lips."

She reached up with a finger and touched my bottom lip. Still there as far as I could tell. The face in my mirror has never looked the same.

"Are you going to ask me? You haven't asked me." Livia never seemed to hold to a subject for long. She cocked a hip and jammed a fist on it.

"Ask what? More of my flaws?"

Her eyes filled with mischief and she gave me a once over. She laughed. "No more flaws. Really. I meant about what happened in the Handmaiden's garden."

"So," I took a step back and gave her a once over in return. Her lips and her other parts all appeared to be in their right place. No flaws that I could see. "What happened in the garden?"

"Peter died." Livia decided to play.

"What did you see?" I asked.

"I didn't see anything."

"Nothing?"

"I saw the guy I was with. Some men like doing stuff in the shrubbery. Why is that?"

"Did you see...?"

"I'm ready to go back. Let's go back." Livia turned and walked away from me.

"Did you see anyone else out in the garden?" I asked the back of her head.

"No," she said over her shoulder.

Out on the midway, in the glare of a slew of light bulbs dangling over our heads, Bobbie Lee spotted us. He came up toting a funnel of greasy newspaper filled with fried potatoes reeking of malt vinegar.

"Fun, huh?" he leered.

"Yeah," Livia said.

"Did you see the naked lady?"

"Both of them," I put in.

"There were two?"

We laughed at his disappointment.

I dropped Bobbie Lee off at his boarding house, making him promise to not wake up the others renting rooms there. Four old men, two widows, and an over-the-hill actor living out their lives alongside a boy with a secret life.

"You know why you got this job?" Livia said as I unlocked the door to my place. Half the people I knew were hell bent to tell me why I got this gig.

"I was told it was because I was polite and respectful." It sounded silly said out loud.

Livia laughed. "That's not it, you know."

I was getting used to having Livia in my place. The sight of her, the smell of her perfume made it feel less hollow. I hit the switch. Light helped to beat back some of the empty. Livia shot me an odd look as she flounced by me toward the bedroom. A quick penetration with her eyes, a twist of a smile shaping her lips. She had lips and my finger came up to touch where I apparently had none. I shook my head.

"Do you want me to tell you?" Livia asked.

"I guess."

"Come on then," the smile in her voice was music. The walk of her hips was invitation and challenge at the same time.

I was twenty-four that night. The walk of most women's hips usually expressed invitation and challenge. I followed her into the bedroom.

Standing before the dresser, Livia began to shed jewelry, costume stuff, more glitter than value, dumping each bit into one of my cereal bowls.

"You are not here – well, I am here not because you are a God-given gift to proper society, all polite and respectful like you claim."

"No?"

"No." Livia lifted a foot to pull off her shoe. "It's your loyalty, not your manners."

"My loyalty?"

"Bet on it," she said, lifting the other foot, then tossing the shoes into a corner.

"How do you figure all that?"

"I don't figure it, Conner. I know it." she turned to look at me.

"Then how do you know that?" I asked again, aware that Livia called me by what I thought of as my name and not Paddy.

"I know it from Rose Maceo's own lips. I listen," she said. "You know that the Maceo brothers host poker games. High stake poker games."

I nodded. It was common enough knowledge. The games were never for locals, certainly not low rollers, and by invitation only. The buy in was supposed to be huge.

"Well, along with first class booze and fancy food, Sam brings in a few girls. Pretty ones. Classy ones."

"And you were one of those girls?"

Livia got a hurt look on her pretty face. "I can be classy if I want to."

"No. No." I put up my hands defensively. "You are nothing but class, darlin'. Swear."

That seemed to soothe her.

"Anyway, we'd get there early to help set up." Livia took a step toward the bed still facing me and bent over.

My heart thumped. The girl reached up under the short flapper skirt, took hold of a pair of even shorter and ruffled bloomers, dragging them down to her knees. She straightened and let them drop around her ankles.

I can't remember exactly, but I think I remember the corner of Livia's lips raise in a satisfied smirk. She stepped out of them. A toe kicked the bloomers over onto her shoes. She turned and sat on the edge of the bed to regard me with those big dark eyes.

"We got to hear things. The help is always invisible," she said.

No one could ever convince me that Livia could be invisible. My voice box froze up. I wouldn't be able to speak if the house was on fire.

Livia chuckled. She leaned back to prop herself on her elbows and stretched out her legs to rest them on her stockinged heels.

Mary the Mother, that girl had legs. From there to the floor and back again. Not ol' stick legs either. Woman legs with some meat on them, thighs molded with true art, knees sculpted by the loving hand of God Almighty. The Lord loved women and I thanked him for it.

Livia laughed again. "Like them? I knew you were a leg man."

My eyes followed them from trim ankles, long shins, perfect knees, stocking tops pulled tight and rolled into garters, solid thighs, all the way to that dark glisten where those legs met. Then, finally, back to the amusement in her eyes. I could only nod.

She sat up, pulling her feet back beneath her.

"Come here," she said.

I just stood there. Mostly because I was stunned. However, some sense of duty rose in me. She was my charge. My orders were to take care...

"Come here." It was more an order this time.

I was twenty-four. I stepped close to her. She reached up to fiddle with my belt.

"I should not be doing this," I managed.

"You're not doing it. I am."

THE CHIEF

"SORRY," LIVIA CAME INTO THE KITCHEN, BLINKING AT THE sunshine streaming through the window.

"Nothing for it."

"You sure?" She drag-heeled over to the coffee cup I'd set out for her. "How do you feel this morning?"

"Rode hard and put up wet."

"Sorry," she repeated.

"Thanks anyway. For last night, I mean."

"I didn't do it for you. I did it for me."

"Either way," I said.

Nothing else to say. I got the feeling that's where it was going to be left. Probably a good thing.

I heard a series of knocks. Little Porky on the job. Livia's eyes questioned me.

"I figure it's Bobbie Lee," I said. "He's about due."

"Damn. I'm for a bath."

The water was running before I heard the clatter on the stairs. Two people. My hand wrapped around Rose Maceo's pistol in my jacket pocket.

Bobbie Lee's smiling face peeked through the door. Bleary-eyed Manny Dents followed him in.

"Jesus, that little toad lets anybody up those stairs," I joked.

"Gotta get some class in this joint somehow," Bobbie Lee returned.

"What the hell are you doing here, Manny?" I asked pulling my hand from my jacket pocket. He looked a wreck after duty on the Seawall all night.

"No rest for the innocent. Rose wants somebody with your damsel-in-distress. That gets to be me."

"You gonna be okay?"

"I'll be jake. Grab me some sleep on your couch."

I just shook my head.

"Where is that damsel?" Bobbie Lee asked.

"Bath."

"Don't guess we can wait so I can say hello?"

"Sorry, Bobbie Lee," I said. His smile faded.

"I'll give her a hug from you," Manny offered.

"Be nice, now," Bobbie Lee said.

"God, I will. Rose don't like upsetting women."

Shit. I cleared my throat and hoped the boys didn't hear. "Let's do it."

There was no real title, no sign over the door for the loose association of Negro dock workers. The office was tucked into the corner of the red brick commercial building two blocks down from the Galveston wharves.

Faded, shabby, worn, typical office. The front area had three rows of beaten up, wooden, unmatched kitchen chairs waiting for unoccupied dock workers. A chewed up bannister separated the chairs from three cluttered desks. A map of the city docks, specs really, was nailed to the wall behind. Beside it a door led to an inner sanctum. The ruling roost of Jasper "Chief" Higgins.

Chief Higgins leaned against the door jamb talking to another man sitting at one of the desks.

"Mr. Higgins?" I asked as I entered.

"Yeah, suh. I'ze cumin'. Directly, suh," Higgins toned. It didn't sound right coming from this mountain of a man. He gave a nod at the man at the desk, who began to shuffle through a stack of papers. Higgins straightened. "Wat ya'll needin' frum me, mistah?"

It was too early for this crap. "You can drop the Sambo routine, Mister Higgins. I know you."

Higgins gave a glance to his friend. The paper shuffling ceased.

"I don't know you, suh," Higgins said. His rich Negro baritone remained, the slave jive left. "How do you know me?"

"Well, I know your voice. Out of the night. The dark. Down at the west end siding." That's where we stowed liquor into train cars for smuggling north.

"Ah. Beach or Town?" Higgins bobbed.

He'd bring his crew out into the night, working for extra money. And why not. We'd have folks helping his men stash our liquor aboard ships. It was nice to know that both Galveston's gangs accepted his help.

"Beach," I answered.

"Cousin?" Higgins said over his shoulder. "Go get some breakfast."

The man dropped the papers in his hand and left the building. Higgins followed him up to the front window. "That boy out in the car belong to you?"

"Yeah."

"What does the Beach want with me?"

"The Beach? Not much. But I want to ask you about Peter Godines."

"Godines? Good man. I'm gonna miss him." Higgins stared out the window.

Good man? I didn't want him to be a good man. I wanted him to be a man due a murdering.

"He was your lawyer?" I asked.

"Not just mine."

"He was more than that, I hear."

"Jobs. Jobs can be pretty important. Especially for the Negros."

"I heard he got ya'll to work for less money."

"No. He didn't. That was me. I made that deal with him."

"Good Lord, why?"

"Ain't it clear? I did it 'cause less of something is better than more of nothing."

"Ya'll must've caught hell from the white dock workers."

"Massah, we be darkies," Sambo returned to Higgin's mouth. "Hellfire be all round us darkies. All the time."

I laughed. Couldn't help it. "Working's better than not."

"Food on the table beats none."

"Tell me, did Godines catch hell too?"

"Godines liked hell. Sniffed after trouble like it was a woman and he was a sailor on leave. Why does the Beach want to know about all this?"

I studied Chief Higgins for a moment. I knew his story. A sailor in his younger years, who achieved the rank of First Mate or Chief Officer. In the night as I hauled crates of liquor from truck to freight car, I heard him say a Chief Officer's main duty is to the correct storage of the cargo. Who better to be in charge of dock workers doing just that. He sure knew how to stow stuff in rail cars. He was undisputed boss of all the Negro dockhands.

My options for answering his questions floated in and out as I listened. Who did want to know about Peter Godines? Rose Maceo? The Handmaiden? Why does anyone want to know? What of any of this could I say to Chief Higgins?

I walked to the window. "I'm here to find out who killed Godines."

"I didn't kill him."

"You know if he has any enemies?"

Higgins laughed, a deep growl of a laugh. "Godines was a lawyer."

"Recent enemies?"

"Direct, personal enemies? Not really. None that I know of. But, I got the idea that he and his boss had a falling out."

"Over what?"

"Something his company wanted to do at the wharf." Higgins said. "Trying to get with the city to expand."

"The company wanted to enlarge the port?"

"No. It was Godines wantin' it."

Interesting. Curious, but interesting. "Was the shrimp fleet tangled up in this?"

"How did you know?"

"Something I heard." That was only half true. "What was their beef?"

"The commercial port gets built up using city money. Not so with the shrimp fleet. Those boys foot the bill," Higgins said.

"So?"

"So, extending the port means pushing the shrimper's piers into the bay."

"And no one's gonna help out the shrimpers."

"You catch on quick – for a Beach thug," Higgins said with no particular animosity.

"This dock problem, big enough for somebody to murder over?" I asked.

"Son, my preacher always told me that no man truly knows what's in the heart of men," Higgins rumbled. "But, that might not be true of the shrimper's preacher."

I looked him in the eye. "What's that supposed to mean?"

"The Reverend Hollis Love might be a special case. For a preacher named Love, the man knows something about hate."

I let out an exasperated breath, wanting more.

"I think I'll let you ask around," Higgins added. "Talk about something else."

Well hell. I let out another puff of breath. Higgins stood unmoved.

I slid behind the wheel.

"It did not go well?" Bobbie Lee asked.

"Went okay." Maybe. I squinted against the sunshine.

"Then why the frown? The Chief have some answers?"

"Some."

"Then, who killed Godines?" Bobbie Lee pushed the starter for me, tired of waiting.

I shook my head. "He gave me a couple of names. I figure that's two more than I had when I woke up."

"Of course, he claimed he didn't do it." Bobbie Lee nodded.

"That's what he said."

"He might be lying."

"He might be." I steered the Studebaker away from the docks.

"So, let's keep him on the list. That makes three. Four, if you ask me."

"Four?"

"I still vote for the wife. Anybody I know got shot back home, 'sides a bootlegger, got shot by a wife or a husband," Bobbie Lee said.

I gave him a look.

Bobbie Lee continued. "Who did he say killed him?"

"Higgins didn't say killed. He just told me who was mad at him."

"Jesus, that was some kind of mad," Bobbie Lee said with a faraway look. I got the idea he pictured Godines, a rag piled on the flagstones of the Handmaiden's garden.

"Don't know if they're the ones. Either of them."

"So, again, who do we got for Godines' murder?"

"One of 'em's his boss."

"Who is?"

"I don't know his name or I don't remember it."

"The other?"

"I figure we'll find him today. Give him a visit."

"Do you know his name?"

"Reverend Hollis Love," I answered.

Bobbie Lee's silence made me glance at him. Jaw slack. Eyes big as pie plates.

"Merciful God. You don't mean it?" he said.

"Well, I thought I did." What the hell is the problem with a damn preacher?

"You know who he is, right?"

"No."

"Hollis Love is some kind of Grand Pooh Bah of the Ku Klux Klan."

"You're stringin' me."

"Am not. That's the dope. Straight up," Bobbie Lee assured.

Could this day get any better? I touched my empty shirt pocket. "Gotta deck?"

Bobbie Lee nodded.

"Light me up?" I asked.

Bobbie Lee fished out his pack of Luckys, lit one and jammed it in my lipless mouth. I left it there, squinting from the smoke roiling up into my eyes.

The races were more or less at peace on the Island. The biggest problem was the black troops that sometimes got trained over at Fort

Crockett. That was when they got drunk rowdy on weekend leave. I had the local Klan figured as some sort of twisted masonic lodge that spent its time railing in favor of States' Rights and reliving the past glories of the dead Confederate States of America.

I smiled to myself. Some of those oldest Klansmen probably beat war drums in line of march with Rebel regiments. Maybe one or two with my old man's division.

"Finding something funny?" Bobbie Lee asked.

I took the butt from my mouth and put the hand on the steering wheel. "Not a damn thing. But this stinking pile just got serious."

"Piles of serious. That'd make me smile." Bobbie groused, not meaning it.

"A rich businessman with a grudge. A rabid preacher hatin' folks that don't stick to their race. An ice box of a wife. Jesus!"

"I don't think we should take the Chief off the list either. What do you want to do?"

"Don't know. Rattle some cages. Stomp on in and start wailing away on 'em. Get some answers."

We thought about it over lunch. Nobody got rattled or wailed on that day.

Next day Papa Regelo gave us the name of Peter Godines' boss. We found Papa, and our replacement boys, collecting from the machines in a car repair shop off 34th Street.

Papa had been around. Seen some stuff. The slots concession had been a kind of semi-retirement gift from Ollie Quinn, boss of the Beach Gang. One thing good about the Beach Gang, they could, mood striking them, take care of their own. I thought he might advise me in my time of need.

I didn't have anywhere else.

We walked up to Papa and his new boys. Him in his usual oversized brown slacks, gold-rimmed glasses, and white shirt whose sleeves were secured by garters. The new boys a rag tag of knickerbockers, charity shirts, newsboy caps, and no socks. I gave him a nod to take a stroll with me and left Bobbie Lee sitting in the shade on the running board of Papa's truck.

I explained my problem when we found our own shade under a scraggly oak a half block down.

"Bobbie Lee said we should just stomp in and start beating answers out of 'em," I added.

Papa chuckled. "You know, he may be half right."

"Yeah?"

"Sometimes yeah, sometimes no. You say there are two people might've done it?"

"If you don't count the man's wife."

"With the wife – sometimes no," Papa said. "Who are the two men?"

"One's Godines' boss. Seaway Shipping."

"I know him. Or, I know of him. Name's Ney. Frank Ney."

"How do you know him?"

"His company owns a string of little stores. You've been to a couple. They have our machines," Papa said. "What makes you think he might've done the man in."

"Something to do with the port."

"Ney and the stiff fighting over something at the port?"

I had to shrug. "All I know is that Godines wanted to grow it."

Papa got a strange look on his face.

"What?" I asked.

"You know about the Sealys and the Moodys?"

"Not really."

"They got this feud going. Been going on forever," Papa said.

"Over the port?"

"Not just that. Over every damn thing. Did Godines side with the Moodys?"

"I'm told he wanted the port to grow. Thought it was more about something else. You think joining the Moodys would earn him a murdering?"

It was Papa's turn to shrug. "Don't know. Who else you got?"

"You got a fag?" I asked.

"Same dumb Paddy." Papa shook his head. "You know you can buy these things. Two bits a deck."

He took out a crumpled pack from his pants pocket and handed it over. I managed to pull out an undamaged Lucky, straightened it out best I could, and snatched out a box of matches from my own pants.

"Hey, I got my own matches," I lied. They were Bobbie Lee's, borrowed this morning. Took me three of them to light the damn Lucky. "The other one I got is Reverend Hollis Love."

Papa Regelo laughed out loud. The phlegmy, barking laugh of an old man with a lifetime of bad habits. The laugh ended in a fit of pregnant coughing.

"Hellfire Hollis, that ol' Flim Flam. Why the hell would that grifter want the likes of Peter Godines dead in his grave?"

"Heard that he didn't like the way Godines messed around with colored women. Him being a Klansman and all."

"A rabid Klansman, huh?" Papa sniggered. I saw the skepticism in his eyes.

"Godines also helped a lot of negro dockworkers find work."

"So?"

"So, what I read in the papers."

"The Klan causing grief in the papers?" Papa asked.

"It's what I read." I said.

"Any of that grief happening on the Island?"

I thought about it. No. I shook my head.

"I've known that old bastard, Hollis, since he showed up here. Ten years ago. Eleven. He'd been chased out of some town or other. His game was conning widows out of their money back then."

"He liked the rich widows a lot?" I asked.

"They didn't have to be rich. If those poor petticoats had a dollar in a cookie jar, ol' Hellfire'd kiss it out of 'em," Papa said. "Met his match though."

"Yeah?"

"Mrs. Reverend Maddie Greyson Love, dead these many years.

But that royal bitch dog took up the good Reverend's hand and taught him the Big Con. The biggest cons."

"The God Con?"

"Among others. The Badger. Maddie was a pretty enough piece, with the morals of a March hare. She'd squirm around joyfully with well-to-do married men. Then ol' Hellfire'd threaten to take proof to the wife. They'd do the Fiddle game. Maddie'd leave a fake Ming vase as a collateral on a debt with Hellfire and the mark. Hellfire'd vouch for its value, then sell his half of the proceeds. The mark'd never see the two of them again. They just had a gay ol' time."

"Mr. Quinn let him get away with all that?"

"Maddie and Hellfire weren't idiots. Quinn got his cut."

"So, the church?"

Papa laughed. "You know, Maddie was no one trick pony. She could squirm good, but she could hear good too. And Hellfire Love knew how to spin a tale. She got him doin' the Tent Meeting circuit. He did the Bible thumpin'. She passed the collection plate."

I flicked the butt into the gutter and chewed at my bottom lip. I did have a bottom lip, even if Livia couldn't see it.

"The Klan?'

"Came with the church after a while," Papa said. "Parishioners. The Klan's got its own collection plate. You really don't know what to do, do you?"

He took out his wad of smokes, straightening out a couple. He handed me one, stuck the other between his teeth, then pulled out his lighter. That Austrian job, made from a spent bullet shell with a striking wheel, snapped some fire, lighting the two butts.

"What to do? That's half the reason I came to see you." I dragged large at the cigarette and made a glance at Bobbie Lee.

He had Papa's new boys pitching pennies at the wall across from the truck. Hoped those boys liked empty pockets. My good friend rarely lost at that game.

"Let me ask you, Conner, how long you been here?" Papa asked.

"A couple of years."

"Up on the mainland, you bootlegged?"

I nodded.

"How long?"

"Three. Four years."

"I think you know how to get what you want. You've seen how men like us do it," Papa said. I gave a half-committed twist of my head. "Rose Maceo tells it. Sometimes ask. Sometimes deal. Sometimes push. Sometimes make 'em bleed. It's all in the sometimes."

"What time's which?" I asked.

"Don't know. Do know a couple of things, though," Papa started. "Ney's a businessman. Been in it awhile. As far as I know. More money than God. Might wanta start low and work your way up."

"Sounds like good advice."

"And the good Reverend is a con artist through and through. Can't con a con. Mean what you say. Sooner than later he'll bluff. Call his bluff."

"Got it," I said.

"No you don't. Watch him close. You know Sammy Mustard over at the Martini Theatre?"

I didn't.

"Used to call Love 'the Otter.' You know about otters?"

I shook my head again.

"Otters are cute as new born kittens. Get up under their fur and they're meaner than stepped-on copperheads."

BESS

I knew how to get what I wanted. That's what Papa said. I didn't know what that meant.

"Do you know what he meant?" I asked Bobbie Lee as I drove back toward downtown.

"He meant we should feed folks some knuckles. Do some batting practice." Bobbie Lee nodded with a grim smile. "Folks'll be tellin' us all we want to know."

"More likely telling us anything they think we want to hear."

"They'll think we want to hear who the hell killed that stiff."

"And, in an hour or two, we'll have all three of them swearing they're the killers if we'd stop. How much thumping could you take before you'd be telling me anything I wanted to hear."

"More thumpin' than you, I bet."

I looked at his blonde, determined little head. "You know, I bet you could at that."

No doubt of that. My, idiot, stubborn friend. A man could lop off parts of him all day. That bastard would grin and use his last breath to spit in his tormentor's eye.

Lazy that afternoon, I didn't feel like swinging fists or swinging bats. Instead, I stopped at the Galveston News office. The Godines took the paper. We drove to see Mrs. Godines.

The neighborhood's substance spoke of the Island's wealth. Victorian. Georgian. Built solid. Built up on brick pilings with columns, facades, gables, scroll work, gingerbread. Mrs. Godines kept house in what I called a cracker box. A very pretty cracker box two stories high, painted yellow with white trim. Three stories if you counted the scroll-worked widow's walk of a crown.

Norfolk pine graced its corners – an emerald green shawl. Azalea and roses hid the raised foundation but barely concealed the statue of Mother Mary to the right.

I stopped before the two cast iron fences separating the house from the street. The gate of the inner fence, standing taller than me, was closed. The outer fence, of spear-point bars, barely reached my knees. An illusion. The fence once stood tall, guarding another house that stood on this site before the great hurricane. Before the city fathers raised up the entire city with sand dredged from Galveston Bay. Many such fences still thrust themselves through the new sand.

There was much to envy in such a house. Maybe also in such a man that once lived in it. I guessed that, as an ambitious man, I might envy Peter Godines. But I am not particularly ambitious. And Peter Godines left this earth gurgling away his life on the back path of a whorehouse.

I opened the man's gate and took the climb to his front door. Bobbie Lee didn't like being left in the car, but I made the climb alone.

The demon maid answered my knock.

"I will see Mrs. Godines," I said into her glare.

"This house is not open to the likes of you, trash," the woman, Dora, said.

"Is she at home?" I asked, making sure I looked her in the eye.

"Don't matter to you, boy."

"I'm gonna have to insist." I held her eyes in my gaze. That was one way I've seen men get what they want.

The two of us had a stare-down. I admit I was surprised when Dora wavered.

"I will see if Mrs. Godines is receiving this morning."

The door closed. I stood there wishing for a stronger breeze. Bobbie Lee grinned at me when I glanced over my shoulder. His grin broadened when I flashed him an obscene gesture.

A muffled argument seeped from the house. Women's voices. I could not make out the words. A longer time than I wanted passed before a clatter of footsteps that I felt as much as heard. The door parted, barely. Dora's eyes threw daggers.

"Mrs. Godines will see you." She disappeared, leaving me to push the door open.

The interior matched the exterior. A comfortable and elegant Victorian. I got the feeling, however, that it was set up for entertaining more than living. The entry stretched deeply into the house. To the left, the dining room with its mahogany china cabinets and long, heavy table seating fourteen. On the right, a study crowded with plush, over-stuffed seating and a simple enough desk at the front window.

Dora allowed me my look at the two rooms then turned to lead me, at a march, deeper into the house to the library. A place for more intimate, more private, entertaining. I thought that's where I'd be planted. Instead, Dora gestured the other direction. A parlor. Less masculine. A sitting room for afternoon teas. Opposite the entry, a half-round sunroom faced the side gardens.

"Mrs. Godines will be down," Dora said. Abrupt might well describe her leaving.

I was left to stew.

Above me, floorboards creaked as someone moved back and forth across the floor. Dishes rattled and clanked in the kitchen at the back of the house. Finally, heeled shoes knocked their way down the stairs. I rose from the couch.

Mrs. Godines entered with curiosity on her face and a quirk of a smile. She was a handsome woman, sternly sculpted nose and chin.

Full lips. Rich cream skin. She wore a pale linen dress with short sleeves, a thigh length, gauzy jacket, each decorated with a light blue lattice stitching.

"Dora told me that the riff-raff from the funeral home was here to see me."

"I'm sorry to disturb you," I lied. "Is this not a good time?"

"No, no. I'm afraid new widows have a lot of time. You will take tea?"

I nodded, welcoming the invitation because I didn't think she would be so happy for long.

"I think it is me who must apologize to you," Mrs. Godines went on. "I know I'm not properly attired. I'm afraid I do not own so many black dresses. I'm forced to – well, I apologize."

Actually, I had the distinct impression the lady fished for a compliment. "Your dress is quite fetching."

Mrs. Godines didn't blush exactly, but her lips twisted into a barely discernable smile.

"I don't know your name." She looked into my eyes.

"Conner Miles, ma'am. They call me the Conner. Conner."

"Why are you at my home, Mr. Miles?"

Dora chose that moment to stomp into the room. A tray of cups, cream and sugar servers, and a tea pot rattled in her hands. She sat it on the table, all the while glaring at me.

"Thank you, Dora," Mrs. Godines said. The maid straightened. "That will be all. All, Dora."

Dora took a long count before she stepped away. I caught a hiss from her as she left. "Trash."

"We will sit for our tea, I think." Mrs. Godines gestured toward the couch. "How do you take yours, Mr. Miles?"

"Poured," I answered. That brought another smile.

She handed me the filled cup as I sat, then poured her own. She surprised me when she sat on the couch with me.

"I'm due an answer, I believe." Mrs. Godines half-turned to face me, threw an arm up on the back of the couch, and placed her chin on her palm.

"I want to know who hurt your husband," I said, my tea untouched.

"Who killed Peter, you mean?"

"Yes, ma'am."

"You do not have to couch your language with me, young man. I'm no gilded lily. I will do the same for you," Mrs. Godines said. Then she proved it. "I suspect that you do not want to know who killed Peter. I suspect it is your boss that wants to know that."

True enough. Mrs. Godines reached over to pat my knee. Pat my knee.

"You're just too young," she continued. "Too young to be wanting anything to do with such as this."

That was not true. Well, I was younger than her, but I did want this chore. Realizing that surprised me. I pictured the dead man, a lifeless rag in the Handmaiden's backyard.

"Maybe that is so, ma'am. But I'm the one that's here," I said.

She looked at me a moment.

"What do they want to know?" she asked finally.

"I want to know," I countered. "More about Mr. Godines. His life, I guess. The kind of man he was."

"My husband was a rakehell, but I think you know that. I didn't. Not at first. My fault," she said. "Let me introduce myself to you. A real introduction."

I gave her a shrugging nod. Why not?

"I am Elizabeth Throckmorton Godines. Bess Godines. Do you know of the Throckmortons?"

"Familiar somehow."

"Texas royalty, and proud. My family has been in the State forever. Land. Industry. Government. A good thing – having a Throckmorton in the family."

"You gave Mr. Godines a pass into power here?"

"Not like that. Our families, both of them, saw our marriage as a merging of two powerful families."

"The Godines family?"

"Ancient family. Always in shipping in some way. Once Portugal, with Spain, ruled the world."

"You treated your marriage like that?" I knew that was harsh, but the woman wanted no couched language. The question gave her pause.

"Shall I warm your tea?" she sidestepped.

I took the untouched cup and gave it a tentative sip. Warm enough. I shook my head. Mrs. Godines turned her eyes away and attended her own cup for a while. I figured I would have been booted out of her house for my last question. It set her back some. I began to think that the lady might be wanting some attention. Even attention from such as me. I worked on the tea and waited.

"It was my fault, you know," Mrs. Godines said at last. I almost thought she meant her husband's death. She clarified. "It was my fault he – he strayed."

"Ma'am, you do not need to talk about this."

"And why not, Mister Riff-raff? We are being honest. And I have a side to this story. If you wander around asking about my husband's life, I fear my side will not be heard."

"Then I will take more tea," I said. I gestured down her move toward the teapot and poured it myself. I think I was right. The attention.

"Jake. Isn't that what all the young people are saying? When things are good, I mean." Mrs. Godines did not wait for an answer. "The life of a woman, even a girl, in society is a busy one. As busy as any working man's. Busier."

"I would bet it is," I said, doubting I'd bet on it. Not the wife of a man with Godines' money. Apparently, I was wrong.

"We are raised to it. From the day our mothers drop us into our first patent leather shoes, we are sent into a whirlwind of women's concerns."

"Motherhood, Service, and Propriety."

Mrs. Godines looked at me. "Where did you get that?"

"It's the motto on the crest of the Women's Auxiliary at my mama's church. I think that they spent most of their time on propriety."

"These ladies, and your mother, are very accurate."

"You sound surprised," I said.

"Forgive me. I did not take you for someone of society. Not as my family would measure it. We would not consider others, others of your station, to be – well, to be like us."

"The Women's Auxiliary sounds like you? Like your people?" I asked. Mrs. Godines was a handsome woman, but from that moment I did not like her so much.

"Motherhood, Service, Propriety. Throw in cotillions, and fund raisers, and you've got my life." She shrugged.

Thing was, Mrs. Godines and her society dames sounded just like my mama and her Auxiliary sisters. I didn't like them and I was sure I wouldn't like this bunch here. "Sounds like a busy time."

"It was. It is. Well, it should still be after my mourning time. That's why I think it's my fault. I kept right on with all the things women did after I married," she said. "I don't think I even noticed that Peter felt – felt neglected, until I started to notice how empty the house was on most nights."

I wondered if Peter Godines' absences were late coming or right from the first. I didn't say anything, but I wondered. Bess Godines may not have been a good wife though I doubted if Peter did very much to be a good husband. Maybe that's the way of things with rich people.

"Did the two of you try to make things better? I mean, after you noticed."

Another pause. Maybe her face darkened just a bit.

"No we didn't. I didn't." She refused to meet my eyes.

"It must have hurt you."

"Yes."

"So you just stayed busy?"

More silence.

"I got busier," she said. Her tone hardened. "It was my revenge. Or something like revenge. If he had something better to do, then so did I."

Great revenge. Deny the man the very thing that might have kept him at home. If, that is, Godines was ever the man that wanted to stay at home with Bess Godines.

"Ma'am, excuse me for this, but were you mad enough for more than that revenge?" I asked. I'd had enough.

A glare, hot as Satan's hell, flashed out of her handsome face. But she tamped it down.

"Like murder my loving husband?" Mrs. Godines' voice was ice cold.

"Yes, ma'am. Like that."

"Policemen followed you into the funeral home. I had policemen in my home yesterday. They asked me that. Repeatedly."

I waited. I watched her in silence as long as I could. She beat me. I looked at the floor. "What did you answer?"

"I did not kill my husband, Riff-Raff. Look at me. Does anything you see look like someone who would walk into a brothel and stab my husband in the throat?"

No, Mrs. Godines didn't look the sort to do that. Not at first look. I looked again. She sat on the couch, a coiled snake, venom fairly spitting from those eyes. On second thought, maybe she did look just like such a woman.

NETRODYNE

That was that with Mrs. Godines. Quick enough I was out on the street. Glad of it, frankly.

I picked up some good Irish whisky, pulled from the back room of Hadley's Five & Dime, and went back to my place. Bobbie Lee kept silent on the ride. Probably a response to the look on my face.

"Are you good?" he asked, coming in the apartment behind me. "You just ignored Porky."

"Right as damned rain," I pitched the car keys on the lamp stand by the door and enjoyed the clatter it made.

"The woman gave you a bad time?"

I puffed a breath and thought about that for a second. "Actually, it could have gone a lot worse. But, I tell you, my friend, I didn't like doing it. I didn't like being there. And I didn't like that Mrs. Godines."

"Well, damn." Bobbie Lee raised eyebrows and made a face.

"Damn right."

Bobbie Lee nosed around the house while I took my expensive bottles of Irish goodness to the kitchen. I returned with two glasses too full of the liquor.

"Gee thanks, man!" Bobbie Lee exclaimed, taking a glass from me. "You did notice that Livia's not here?"

"I saw Manny's car gone. He must've taken her somewhere."

"Maybe so," Bobbie Lee said.

"Sit down and drink. It's what I'm gonna do," I told him. Livia and Manny could damn well do what they pleased.

I plopped on the couch in a black mood, nursing my whisky and smoking away the better part of those Luckys I bought. Bobbie Lee cranked up his Victrola, dropped the needle on some Negro woman's Blues, and took his favorite place on the floor by the door. The bluesy thrumming and chesty lilts fit my mood well enough.

Dusk closed in on the day, and my second glass of whiskey ebbed toward empty when Porky's rapping echoed up the woodwork. The clomping of a small herd of hard-heeled shoes pounded up the stairs.

"Livia," I shrugged.

"She brought friends, sounds like," Bobbie Lee said.

"Brought a damn mob." I rose and went to the door. It almost smashed my nose opening to Livia's broad grin.

"Hi, hero," she said, coming in and forcing me back a couple of steps. "I bought you something."

"You bought me girls?" I asked, for a tiny Chinese doll and a tall Negro woman, so black to be nearly midnight blue, came in behind her.

"No, silly. I bought you this." Livia giggled.

Manny came in, his arms full of a dark wooden cabinet about the size of a picnic basket, and decorated with three knobs.

"Good God!" I blurted. "That's a Netrodyne."

"It sure as hell is, you lucky bastard," Manny said. "Somebody clear a space on that table yonder."

Bobbie Lee jumped up and ran over to the small table by the window. "Jesus, radio. Radio!"

He quickly emptied the table of its lamp and over-burdened ashtray. Like a flock of kids on Christmas Eve, the rest of us followed Manny and his load across the room.

"The horn's still down in the Ford." He placed the shiny thing on the table. "Bobbie Lee, come help. There's other stuff."

I squatted down before the magic box, totally enthralled.

"Livia, this is too much," I said.

"Before you say I shouldn't have, I should have. You house me. You feed me. You defend me. You're due."

"But, damn," I turned my eyes from the radio. The Netrodyne was the absolute edge of modern science and I had an idea of what it cost. She must have seen that thought on my face.

"I make good money. It was nothing. Anyway, Manny was with me the whole time. and I wanted to have a party."

Crap, I hadn't even thought about the danger.

"Relax. I'm alive and this isn't prison," she said into my frown. "And I wanted to have a Petting Party."

"What's a Petting Party?" Bobbie Lee asked, entering the apartment. Kind of wondered that myself. He lugged two sacks in his fists.

Livia smiled and ignored him. "Ya'll, this is Mai and Bertie. My best friends. That one heading to the kitchen is Bobbie Lee."

"Bobbie?" Mai asked.

"No, Bobbie Lee. I tried Bobbie but it just doesn't fit. The one with the scowl is the Conner."

"Smile, the Conner," Bertie said in a rich deep voice. We'd call that a whisky baritone up home. "We gotta have nothing but smiles. There's a radio in the house."

Bertie's gleaming smile got my own going. Couldn't help it. "Just Conner. Call me Conner."

"We'll get nothing on it before full dark. There's food in those sacks Bobbie Lee's got. Let's eat," Livia said. The girls and I left Manny and Bobbie Lee trying to work the horn into the new magic chest. It looked identical to the one blooming out of the Victrola. Livia and Bertie started working on the sandwich makings they'd brought from the meat market down the block. I watched them as

Mai poured my Irish and tap water into glasses. Tap water in my Irish. I grimaced.

Bertie and Mai couldn't be more different from each other. Bertie stretched skyward with her long skinny bones. She slicked her short hair to gleam close on her skull and dramatic swirled curls at each temple. I loved her deep resonant laugh and the dignity she showed with every movement and gesture. Mai looked like, and laughed like, she was ten, if you didn't attend her eyes. Those eyes held an all knowing, ancient wisdom. Not like most girls, she wore her hair long. Hair as black as Bertie's, that begged to be touched. I certainly wanted to touch it. I never understood why folks thought the Chinese were yellow-skinned. Mai's wasn't. Maybe porcelain. Maybe the color of the antique organ keys at my mamma's church. Flawless.

The three women, heart-breakers all, brought food and drink to the table and sat around me. A sandwich for each of us, butcher paper for a plate. Another square of the paper held a pile of pickle sticks that were the best I ever tasted. A glass of watered whisky apiece.

Livia let the two girls chortle about how cute they thought Manny and Bobbie Lee were. I watched the show and chewed my sandwich, wondering why I wasn't among the cute. Livia must have read that on my face.

She put a hand on my neck and leaned close to my ear. "Don't worry, Conner. You're cute, too."

Couldn't help grinning at her.

"What is a petting party?" I repeated Bobbie Lee's question.

"All the kids are doing it. Dancing. Drinking. Laughing. A little kissing. A little cuddling in the dark. You know. Boys enjoying being boys. Girls enjoying being girls."

"Sounds like what the Romans called an orgy," I said. I was an idiot back then, pronouncing orgy with a hard "g". Or-gee not or-jee. Stupid.

"Orgy," Livia corrected. "And, no. Not that. You all just keep your things behind your buttons. We'll keep our things behind our silks. Jake, right?"

"Jake," I consented and hoped for the same from the two other men. "I like your friends, by the way."

"They're cute, yes?"

"They're funny. They're nice."

"They also knew Peter. Mr. Godines." Livia nodded conspiratorially. "Another present for you."

"Mr. Godines?"

Amid her laughter, Bertie must've heard the name.

"What?" she interrupted.

"We were talking about Peter," Livia said.

"Horrible. Terrible. I liked Peter. He didn't deserve to die like that." Bertie plopped down the last bit of her sandwich. I saw the anger on her face as she stared at the debris.

"I liked Peter, too. I cried when I heard. He was a good man," Mai said in her little girl voice.

Livia looked at me, then turned to Mai. "I don't think Mrs. Godines would think he was a good man."

I nodded. Mai's eyes dropped.

"Peter was no better than he ought to be. No worse." Mai said. "He always treated me good,"

"Me, too," Bertie added.

"He bought you stuff?" I asked.

Bertie shot me a look. "More than that. He was kind. Respectful. He didn't treat me like a…"

"Like a whore," Livia finished for her.

"Yeah, like that," Bertie said.

"Me, too," Mai added. "He was nice. He talked with me."

"All our men talk to us, Mai," Livia said.

"Not to me. Not bitching about their wives or their jobs. He talked with me. Like people talk with each other. Like regular people do."

"How did you get tied up with Mr. Godines, Mai?" I asked. I guessed that Bertie worked the brothels. Mai, I didn't know about.

For some reason, Mai giggled. "The Handmaiden would send for me when Peter wanted a China girl. At first. Then Peter would ask for me special."

"Before you ask," Bertie interrupted. "I met Peter over at Belle's Place. On a Thursday night. White folks get to come on Thursdays. Lots of you white folks like the music over there."

"I do," I admitted.

"I seen you there a couple of times." Bertie grinned as if she caught me out.

"What ya'll are calling the Blues…"

"Tell me, Bertie, Who do you think killed Peter?" I asked.

Her face lost its expression. "Somebody that sure hated him. Somebody that wanted him embarrassed. The Handmaiden's back lot, for God's sake."

"Peter ever talk about somebody like that?"

Bertie shook her head.

"Somebody beat him up once," Mai said. "Hit him, anyway. He had black eyes and his nose was all swollen up."

"He tell you what happened?"

"No. All he said was that it was the risks of the trade. Whatever that meant."

"Someone at his work? A man?"

"I don't know if it was a man. Most likely though."

"What makes you think that?"

"My Zumu, my mother-in-law, once told me men stab, women poison."

"She knows that, does she?" Bertie challenged.

Mai smirked. "My Zumu had five husbands. Some of them were younger than her."

Watch out for Mai's Zumu, I thought.

"Well, the women where I come from'll stab 'em quick enough.

Or else they'll pitch a pot full of boiling grease on 'em quicker than hell," Bertie said.

Grim enough, but I had to laugh. More than one man up home got a lap full of frying chicken.

"Women are the worst of all animals," I said.

"We are?" Livia asked, but I got the idea that she might actually agree with me.

"You ladies are not helping," I said.

"I don't think a woman would sneak through the night to a whorehouse and find a way to stab a man in the throat with an icepick," she asserted. The other two nodded agreement at that.

The kitchen door burst open. Bobbie Lee's smile beamed into the room.

"Hey! We think we got Chicago on the radio. Chicago, by God!"

The girls fled into the front room to see the new miracle there. So much for Peter Godines.

Night. I hadn't noticed. The small bulb on the ceiling glared heroically, a weak sepia swath of light across everyone's back. We gathered around Manny as he knelt before the radio. It gurgled, squealed, and spat, as he worked the dial. A red glow reflecting off my wall surprised me. I took a peek. A grilled vent on the radio's back let me see the glass tubes inside. If there was magic in this box, it resided there.

I became a believer when the box spoke. A man's voice speaking in the measured patter of a freak show barker.

"...sounds of the Todd Rivers Orchestra - brought to you – from the Roosevelt Hotel – uptown Chicago. Show us how it's done, Todd!"

Manny grinned. Jazz, frantic and shrill. The three women broke into wild gyrations on the instant. Manny, Bobbie Lee, and I joined in. Well, I did the best I could. The Chicago tower left the Hotel Roosevelt at the top of the hour. Reverend Somebody-or-other replaced the music and started railing us on the wages of sin.

"That's all right, preacher. I'm already goin' to hell," Manny said, reaching for the radio dials.

"Who was it said, heaven for the weather, hell for the conversation? Or something like that," Mai said, earning more than one raised eyebrow. She stuck her pretty, pink tongue out. "Can't help it. I was good in school."

An educated whore, cute as a button. Who'd've thought.

I took a swipe at the sweat on my forehead with the back of my hand and staggered over to the couch, within reach of the watered down Irish. Manny breezed through the radio's settings with its scattering of classical music, old western ballads, preachers, and news. Livia cozied up close beside me.

"Like your present?"

"I do," I told her and enjoyed the reward of her smile.

She took a hold of my wrist and moved my arm to drape around her shoulder. We sat, listened, and watched. Before too late in the evening, long tall Bertie draped herself across Manny's lap, in my one chair. Mai sat on the floor, pressing shoulders with Bobbie Lee. The two of them, after the radio stations signed off, took turns playing Bobbie Lee's Victrola. The last of my Irish made the rounds.

There may have been petting at Livia's Petting Party, but the three girls finally drifted into my room. I fell asleep, alone on the couch, imagining how they crowded into my bed.

A noise woke me. What was it? The milkman? The newspaper boy? I opened eyes to see Manny looking at me, alarmed. He slumped in my chair, feet resting on the coffee table, where he'd spent the night. Whatever the noise was woke Bobbie Lee as well.

The front door banged open and the heavy thumps of many shoes thundered from the stairs. The three of us stood.

A fist pounded on the door. And again. Again. My bedroom door opened. Livia appeared. She held my pistol on her palm as if it was a platter of canapés.

More pounding.

"Police! Open up! Open the door!"

I held up a restraining gesture and was relieved when she backed into my room, shutting the door behind her. Manny and Bobbie Lee jumped into action. They'd both been there before. Each gathered up the booze bottles and glasses, heading for the kitchen. Getting anything illegal out of sight.

Continuous rapping made hollow echoes against the wood. "Police! We know you're in there. Open the door."

I yanked my shirttail from my pants and unbuttoned most of the buttons. One last look around. No visible bottles or glasses. Bedroom door closed. Manny giving me a last look as he shut the kitchen door. Everything as ready as we could make it in a few seconds. I opened the door and began to button my shirt as if I'd just put it on.

A short balding man with a heavy paunch and cheap suit stepped, uninvited, into the room. Two taller, younger, street cops followed.

I'd been there before too. I gave them room. Cops, many of them, seemed like they had something to prove. They made a habit of throwing their weight around. They couldn't help it. A smart Irishman lets them.

The short, stubby one marched toward me. I back peddled. He kept coming. I kept retreating.

"You Miles? Conner Miles?"

"Yes, officer." Not yes, sir. Yes, officer. They liked that.

"I'm Lieutenant Drummer. I'll be talking, so you be listening."

He got a silent nod from me.

"You got Mrs. Godines upset. That means she got my wife upset. My wife got me upset. I don't like being upset, so here I am." Drummer poked a finger onto my chest. "To see to it I don't get upset anymore. Clear?"

I figured I ought to still listen, so I nodded again.

"Then Mrs. Godines won't be seeing you again. More important, I won't be seeing you again, right?"

I fixed my gaze on the center of the cop's forehead and nodded.

Not at the wall to appear indifferent. Not in his eyes to appear challenging. The kitchen door popped open. Manny took a step in.

"You ready for some eggs, Conner?" he asked. He took a look at Drummer and the finger that poked my chest. "Morning, Lieutenant."

Drummer's eyes widened. "This man a friend of yours, Dents?"

I saw Manny's eyes flicker at the use of his hated nickname.

"Yes," Manny answered. "The Conner's a friend. Problem?"

Drummer's finger dropped.

"No. No problem. My business is settled. Isn't it?" Drummer looked back at me. I felt he asked for assurance. Manny unsettled the man.

I remained silent but, for the first time, I looked directly in his eyes.

THE COPPERS MADE AS MUCH NOISE GOING DOWN MY STAIRS AS they did coming up. To my surprise, I was more puzzled than angry at Drummer's excuse of a rousting. I stared at the closed door.

"What the hell was that all about?" Bobbie Lee asked.

That's pretty much what I was thinking as I turned to find him and Manny already in the room. Livia, Bertie, and Mai emerged from my bedroom still in slips.

"I think good ol' Mrs. Godines didn't like you paying her a call," Livia said.

"She must not have liked you one little bit, bless her icebox of a heart," Bertie said.

Bobbie Lee laughed. "I think the lady might have something to hide. You?"

"I don't know. The woman is a top-drawer bitch. But I don't know." At least, I wasn't sure. Couldn't quite picture the woman in that garden, at that time of night, with her wayward husband. "Bobbie Lee, go home. Get cleaned up. Put on your Sunday suit. I think we'll go downtown this morning."

Bobbie Lee got his own puzzled look, but he nodded. "You got it."

"Ladies, I'm taking a bath. See if you can't get Manny to stir up that bacon." A slew of questions followed me into my room but I shut the door on them.

I mulled my problem as I bathed. Any woman confronting her husband at a whore house ought to be pretty noisy about it. Peter Godines' body was found, and nobody said they heard anything. No sign of a fight like there should be. The killing was quick and quiet.

Bacon smells filled the place as I went in, still in shirt sleeves, to eat Manny's cooking.

Livia opened the kitchen door, holding my suit coat and hat. She'd been trying to get the wrinkles out of it. Me and the coffee cup followed her into the living room.

"Manny thinks Mrs. Godines must have something to do with it. You know, sending those cops over and all. Do you?" Livia asked, helping me with the coat as I juggled the coffee.

"I'm struggling with it, to tell the truth."

"Where are you going today?"

"Think I'll go visit Peter's boss. See what I can find out. Maybe some other folks."

"Conner," Livia tilted her head. "Do you really like the radio I got you?"

"Pretty one, you made me feel like the richest man in the world," I answered. "You couldn't buy me with a month of new moons."

Livia beamed.

Bobbie Lee came up.

"Say bye for me, Livia. And try staying close to the house today. Manny's got chores tonight. He'll have to leave early."

"I'll do it. Anyway, the way he and Bertie's been looking at each other, I'll be boiling your sheets this afternoon."

"Gee, thanks for that picture." I grimaced.

She was still laughing as Bobbie Lee and I left.

I felt aired up like a balloon. Blood throbbed heavily in my throat. Coppers are not my favorite folks. Never have been. Bobbie noticed.

"Nervous?" he asked.

"No. Why?"

"You gotta vein popped out on your forehead."

I shook my head. "Didn't really need that visit this morning."

"Yeah." Bobbie Lee laughed. "Nearly wet myself. Hey though, it's over. We'll just avoid Mrs. Godines."

I wondered about that. The Handmaiden wanted Godines' killer. Rose Masceo, a man I did not want to say no to, a man no one should say no to, wanted that mess cleaned up. Maybe cleaning it up meant keeping the wife on the list. For now.

Attempts to think of something else kept me silent on the drive downtown. I tried, instead, to determine just how to handle Frank Ney. Just what I wanted out of him.

A full confession would do it nicely.

Seaways Shipping lived in an old, ornate, four-story, brick building not too many blocks from the Port. Amid the red bricks, white, Greek-style columns, and cornice work was an insert saying Western Bank Est. 1894. I noticed that the brickwork of the top floor did not match the rest of it. Maybe the top of it got sheared off in the Great Hurricane.

A crisply uniformed, diminutive, old man took us up to the top floor in an Otis elevator. He didn't seem overly impressed with the two of us. But he still had to pump his handle three or four times to level the elevator with the flooring. His two-step effort to draw open the sliding scissor gate and a force down of the door's lever allowed us to exit directly into Seaways' reception room.

I heard a word once. Opulent. Means something like over-dressed with expensive stuff. Marble tile floor. Dark wood paneling. Solid, elaborate couches and chairs, richly carved matching wood, and horsehair covered padding. Two huge, round chandeliers dripping with crystals lit the room.

Behind a massive desk, a pretty, young flapper with bobbed hair and a stylish black-and-white print dress, stood and smiled.

"Welcome to Seaways Shipping. How may I help you?" She

leaned over the top of a perfectly scaled model of a steam transport ship.

"We need to see Mr. Ney," I answered. "Miles and Glover of Coastal Register and Supply."

Anybody that knew anything, knew that Coastal Register supplied Galveston with its slot machines. It also supplied casinos with anything to do with gaming: tables, liquor, chips, whatever. Mister Ney would know the name. Papa Regelo collected for Coastal Register, and I handled money with Papa.

"Do you have an appointment?"

"No, but I'm sure Mr. Ney will see us," I said.

"Make yourself comfortable. I'll go see Mr. Ney."

Bobbie Lee and I watched the well-built young lady cross the room and disappear into the inner offices. She did know how to walk. It's always the hips.

I eyed the over-large portrait on the wall behind the desk after the door closed behind the receptionist. A grand, strapping fellow. European, in a Christmas tree of a uniform bedecked in medals and a huge gold sash. He was dashing in his curly bronze hair and standing cocked to one leg as if to allow his tasseled sword to prop against his hip. Behind him, the artist painted a distant, grassy landscape, the apparent source of a breeze that stirred heavy olive drapes over his right shoulder.

"It's a copy, I'm afraid."

A medium tall, slightly stocky man entered.

"Adequate, but a shadow of the original," the man continued as he came to stand beside me. "Michel Ney, Duc d'Elchingen, Prince de la Moskowa, Napoleon's bravest general and a Marshal of France. Also my fourth great-grandfather. I'm Frank Ney."

Mr. Ney extended a limp hand for shaking but his eyes remained on the portrait of his ancestor.

"Mr. Ney," I acknowledged. This Texas boy didn't have it in mind to be much moved by long-dead royalty. I gave him our names. He led us to his office.

No ancestral portraits decorated the room, but it still spoke of money and power. Ney's paneled desk shone dark and polished, and of the same wood as the girl's out front. And as massive. Behind the desk, a large sectioned window looked out over the Bay. Opposite the desk, a detailed map of the Gulf coast took the place of any French general. Ney gestured us into two plush, padded chairs that faced the desk.

"Now, what does Coastal Register and Supply want with me?"

What did Coastal want with Ney? Not a damn thing. What did I want? How could I get it? I looked at Ney for a moment and hoped he could not see how unsure I was.

"Coastal wants to know about Peter Godines. Anything we can find out about what he had been doing. How he had been doing – before his death."

"And that is your business because?" Ney asked.

"Because we were in the process of negotiating some things between him and our company," I lied.

"Hmm, I was unaware that Seaways was interested in anything Coastal Register could offer us."

"Nothing between us and Seaways. We were early in the negotiations. But, this was something for Mr. Godines. Much like what we do for your stores, sir."

Ney harrumphed a coughing laugh. "He was thinking he could compete with me?"

"I doubt it," I said. Why would he compete since it was a lie anyway?

"You wouldn't feel like telling what Peter was planning?"

So it was Peter now.

I decided to ignore his question and smiled instead. "You and Mr. Godines get competitive now and again? I mean, when not partnering with Seaways Shipping, of course."

"Not particularly." Ney's eyes narrowed.

"So you were with him in his efforts to enlarge the Port facility?"

That seemed to set Ney back. Like that fact was not common knowledge.

He shrugged. "I didn't have to be with him on that. Seaways didn't have to be concerned with that effort."

"I would figure that enlarging the Port would be nothing but a help to your company."

"Ha. Enlarging the Port of Galveston would more likely ruin us."

I let my eyebrows rise. Not too much of a stretch, because what he said seemed contradictory. I waited for Ney to add more.

"Building up the Port is the wrong bet. Anyway, it's never going to happen," Ney continued, his eyes lit with an intense heat.

"Why not? Why is it a wrong bet?"

"Because Galveston's going to lose. It'll be Houston becoming the world class port. Bigger than New Orleans. Mobile. Hell, maybe even bigger than New York."

I shot Bobbie Lee a look. For no good reason, but I did. Lucky break for me. Ney saw the glance and misinterpreted.

"Your damned company talked into something with Peter that hinged on big growth around the Port?" Ney asked. He laughed.

"Maybe. Maybe not." I figured I was on to something. His laugh. "I'm thinking this Port thing is all tangled up with the Sealys and the Moodys. Am I right?"

Ney leaned on his elbows with a smirk. "Maybe. Maybe not."

"Building the port is a pet of the Sealy family. That puts Godines fixed up with them. You partnering with the Moodys?"

"Ha. Nobody partners with ol' man Moody. You serve him. I keep myself independent," Ney said.

"But you're puttin' down on Houston just like the Moodys?"

"Maybe. Maybe not," Ney hedged, with that arrogant sneering smirk.

"Seaways money, too?"

He didn't answer.

"You and Godines got to fighting about that, yeah?"

Ney stared at me a long moment. "What is this? You touching me for killing Peter, bastard?"

"Did you?"

Pure hate colored his eyes. "Go down that path, you piece of manure, and I know people that'll kill you deader than hell."

It was my turn to lean forward. "I think I will go down that way. Did you?"

"Hell no!" Ney retorted. "Remember, deader than hell."

I figured it was time to leave. I stood up. Bobbie Lee did the same. Anyway, I knew the comeback for deader than hell.

"I'll ask you to remember something, Mr. Ney. Coastal Register will take poorly to losing one of its workers."

He calculated for a minute, remembering just who Coastal Register was. Coastal was a who, not a what. Not a company. It was the sole property of Ollie Quinn. And Ollie Quinn was the Beach Gang.

"Someone else got Peter. Not me," Ney said.

"All right. Let's go down that path. If not you, who?"

"Peter liked the colored girls. Maybe one of them got him."

"As far as I can see, no woman or girl of any color hated Godines," I said.

"Except maybe his wife." Bobbie Lee grinned.

"Except her," I muttered.

Ney sat there staring off as if searching for another wrongdoer. "Could be someone else. Somebody that doesn't go for..."

"Somebody that doesn't like mixing of the blood," I finished for him. "Who would that be?"

"It's called miscegenation, thug. Read a book. And how the hell should I know." Some of Ney's defiance returned.

"Thanks. I'll read something. But my money's still on you for Godines. When I see you again, I'm gonna bugger you good."

We jammed on our hats and left blue-blooded Ney staring after us.

Back in the Studebaker, I felt Bobbie Lee stare at me.

"What?"

"So you think Ney did it, huh?" he said.

"How the hell do I know?" I barked.

"You just told him he did it. I heard you."

"He might have." I shook my head. "And he might not have."

"So might Mrs. Godines," Bobbie Lee challenged.

And she might have, for all I knew. My shoulders sagged as we rattled down a crushed-shell road.

"Or a colored concubine. A jealous man. Maybe some damned shrimper. Chief Higgins. For all I know, Livia herself might 'a done it. Damn it all."

"That's right, damn all of it," Bobbie Lee said.

I gave him a look, in case he was funning me. Almost ran off the road.

"A dime to a dollar you want lunch," I said, regaining control of the car.

"So, you do know who you ride with." Bobbie Lee repeated an

old and ongoing joke brought up almost every time I'd act surprised that he was hungry.

We pulled into the Eastside Oyster House. Bobbie Lee had pork belly, mustard greens, and beans. I had German sausage and potato hash. Neither of us wanted any damn oysters in this heat. They had a pail of beer on ice that wasn't too flat. That was nice enough.

"What next?" Bobbie Lee asked after we finished the food, the table had been cleaned, and our second beer sat before us.

"Haven't a guess."

Bobbie Lee scratched his chin. "Maybe we're going at it all wrong."

"I'm opened to just about anything. Throw it at me."

Another scratch at his beardless chin.

"Well, think about it," he started. "I've been watching you go into a lot of front doors."

"I guess that's right."

"So, if we ain't findin' anything through those doors, maybe we should kick in one or two back doors."

I raised up palms, shoulders, and eyebrows in a puzzled invitation for him to say more.

"I've been thinking. We have Mrs. Godines, betrayed and with good reason for seein' him dead." Bobbie Lee held up a finger. Up came another finger. "We have that Frenchie feuding over some money thing. Maybe not as burning a reason as a wronged woman."

He paused for effect. A third finger rose.

"Then we got Chief Higgins' colored men and women that might have a bunch of reasons for wanting him dead."

"Oh now, you think jealousy'd cause that attack? On a white man?"

"Jealousy or scorn. What they say about a woman scorned. Just like Mrs. Godines."

"On a white man?" I repeated.

"Don't matter. Those are all about front doors. I'm figuring the back door."

"I don't get it."

"Those are all folks that are taking it personal. Real personal."

"So?"

"So, what if it's not all that personal?" Bobbie Lee asked. "Maybe there's folks that just don't like people that are like Godines."

"The shrimpers. He's messing with their jobs."

"Or folks that don't like mixing the races. Most everyone we talked to pointed us that way."

I shook my head. "I just figured they were trying to throw us down a false trail."

"Maybe it is. Maybe it'll show a true trail more clearly." Bobbie Lee took another sip of beer. "Who knows? Maybe it's the right trail."

"Finish up. Let's go to church."

Shrimpers. Klansmen. I took Bobbie Lee's word that those both meant Nazarene Reverend Hollis Love. Or so we've been told. I figured the best way to hunt down Rev. Love was to find his church. I wheeled the Studebaker back to the Port and headed west, roughly along the Bay shore.

It wasn't much of a church, but it had an impressive title painted on a wooden signboard by the cast iron gate.

New Zion Temple of the Nazarene.

Rev. Hollis Love – Pastor

Not sure about the Temple bit. Hollis Love's church was a clapboard house, with a white wooden cross above its gable, on a big grassy lot. Rev. Love had big plans. Another bigger structure was under construction next to it. Another clapboard thing but shaped like the letter "T" laid on its side. Its high-pitched roof was being shingled as I drove into the lot.

Love had created a sizable parking area in front of the old house, even laying an inch or two of crushed shell. I avoided pulling up under the shade from some live oak because I didn't want birds to make a mess on the Studebaker.

His roofers, three of them, stopped work to give us hard stares as we walked up to the house. No one answered our knocks.

"Maybe we should look in the other building," I said. Bobbie shrugged.

Hollis Love sat on a work table in the one room shaded by the new roof. His back was to us as he talked to two men. Neither looked like construction workers. One gave a nod to the Reverend toward us.

Hollis Love was in his mid-fifties, maybe a little older, well fed, and in shirtsleeves and slacks. Patent leather shoes, I noted. White hair appeared long at first glance. But it was perfectly trimmed, as if clipped today. Spit curls atop his head allowed a well-placed strand to hang down on his forehead. He had gold-rimmed spectacles pulled down low on his nose that he peered over to look at us.

He stood. "Enter, pilgrims. Sinners are always welcome in God's house."

We two sinners exchanged a glance.

"Mr. Love?" I asked.

"Reverend Love, actually. I am here to offer all men, and women, comfort and guidance. How may I help?"

"You can help by giving me a few moments of your time."

"Given freely, sir. Speak to me." Love shifted on the table to face us.

"Privately, I think."

Love turned, looked over his shoulder, giving a quick smile to the men he'd been talking to. I didn't like that smile.

"The Lord has no secrets, friend." Love turned to me. His friends were not grinning.

"Privately," I repeated. Love, I remembered, was a conman. I didn't think he needed any help from his friends. Especially if he figured to lie to me.

Love studied me a moment, gauging me. Without turning around he made a dismissive gesture towards the two men. We got hard stares from them much like the roofers gave us.

Bobbie Lee, always having my back, drifted after them and closed the door.

"What's this about, youngster?" Love asked.

"The name's Miles."

"Irish boy, huh? That's all right. God's got room for Catholics, too."

I laughed. It wasn't a happy laugh. My momma used to say things like that. "Southern Baptist, really. We haven't been Catholic since before George Washington started wearing long pants."

"What do you want, Southern Baptist Miles?"

"Do you know who Peter Godines is?" I got right to it.

Love thought for a moment, or pretended to. That's the impression I got, anyway. He shrugged and shook his head.

"Deuteronomy 7:3. You shall not intermarry with them," he said.

"Thou shalt not murder," I replied.

Love stood abruptly, anger in his conman eyes. "Thou should know that I didn't kill anybody."

I was about to tell him that I thought he might know who did. Instead, I caught Bobbie Lee dropping his hand into his jacket pocket. An instant later someone behind me slammed a fist into the side of my face.

Through the stars exploding in my head, I saw a guy skidding past me as if he had a running start. His face showed alarm – as if surprised that I was still standing. Well, I'm a cement-skulled Irishman, and my jaw's not made out of glass.

I wasn't a good fighter. Not back then. Good fighters remain clear-eyed and calculating in a fight. They do if they're any good. I rage. I launched myself at him.

Don't remember much about it. The man slapped and clawed at me. I certainly clawed at him. I kind of heard people screaming. Then we were on the floor. I was sitting on his chest, my hands throttled his throat, and his face was a strangled reddish blue.

Things began to clear up.

Bobbie Lee's high-pitched screaming, "Come on! Come on! Do it! Do it! Come on!"

"Mr. Miles? Mr. Miles?" Hollis Love, on his hands and knees, begged, almost softly.

I looked up. The roofers and the two men that had been talking to Love stood, pale-faced and angry, around the room. Bobbie Lee, in a half-crouch, screamed and waved his .38 back and forth, daring them all.

With murder still in my soul. I pushed the man's neck hard against the floor, pulled back my right fist, and hit him hard in the face. Twice.

"Are we done?" I said to him, cocking back that fist for a third punch. "Are we done?"

He didn't reply. I stood up. He rolled over on his side, choking for breath, and pressed a hand to his busted lip.

"Hey! Hey!" I called to Bobby Lee. When he looked at me, I gave a palms-down gesture. He straightened and stopped screaming. The pistol stayed in his hand.

The pain returned. The side of my face felt like a hot, aching piece of meat that didn't belong to me. My skin burned in all the places we had grappled. The knuckles that busted the man's face were bloody and skinned. My jacket's sleeve bunched around my wrist, ripped off in the struggle.

"Damn," I swore and added a few more choice words. "Is that the man that killed Godines?"

I looked down at Love as he helped the guy into a sitting position. "Is he?"

The Reverend looked. He shook the bloodied man until he raised his eyes.

"I swear to God," Love locked eyes on me. "He did not kill Godines. I don't know who did."

"Don't con me, conman. I know who you are and where you came from."

Now Love looked even more shook up than he did before I spoke. He was a conman, however.

"Straight up. I didn't do it. He didn't do it. My people didn't do it."

"The Klansmen didn't?"

"No. I'd 'a known," he said. That part I think I believed. The Klan's another gang. Boss has gotta okay things like that. Of course, I was told he was the boss Klansman.

"Shrimpers?"

After a pause, Love answered. "They didn't like him much. But not all shrimpers go to my church."

Or marched with your Klan, I speculated. I let out a breath. Damn, my jaw hurt.

"Here's some gospel, Reverend. If you are, in any real way, a shepherd to your flock, you mail that bastard you're holding out of town. I see him again, he's gonna be mutton on a spit." I turned to the others and raised my voice. "I'll be leaving now. Here's two things to chew on. Anybody follows us out gets a hole shot in 'em. And, anyone getting' bright ideas can come find me. I'll be at the beach. The Reverend can tell you about that. So, all of you try not to be as stupid as you look."

FIGHTING HURTS. FIGHTING HURTS EVEN WHEN YOU WIN. THE next morning I found pain in places I didn't know I had. My jaw, of course. Both knees, an elbow, my left big toe, my lower back.

I let Livia take care of me. She wasn't very good at it.

She wrapped my busted up hand in too much gauze and used more of it to tie the thing off. I listened to her, and wondered about her when she went to the ice box to chip off bits of ice with an icepick. Then I'd groan when she came back with her chips bundled in a towel, to press hard onto my swollen jaw. The mushy food she made, in deference to my latest chewing skills, wasn't all that great either.

She looked good doing all this, though.

Bobbie Lee showed up early. He had Mai and two bottles of Irish in tow. He left the two bottles but took Mai, his Victrola, and the keys to the Studebaker. Rain was on the way and he didn't want to get caught in it.

They weren't to the end of the block before the rumble of thunder rolled in from the Gulf. A new breeze brought smell of rain, salt air, and wet growing things.

At first, heavy drops splattered at the roof and walls. I closed the windows behind the Netrodyne to keep it dry. Rain closed in so that I barely made out the houses down the way. Thunder and lightning played war in the sky. Deafening and brilliant.

Livia and I sat on the couch and watched, awed and silent.

"When I was a little thing, this kind of storm scared me silly. All us girls at the orphanage squealed and grabbed on to each other. Made it worse than it was, everybody feeding on each other's fear." Livia shuddered and leaned over against my ribs.

I put my arm around her, pressing the bandaged hand against her arm. "They're headed inland. It'll be over soon."

"I hope so."

"I can pull the drapes. We don't have to watch."

"No. Don't. It's near as good as moving pictures. I'll get you some more ice." Livia grabbed up my wounded hand and removed my arm. I managed not to wince.

I did flinch when she returned and pressed the bundle against my face.

"I'm sorry," she begged, still leaning over me.

My eyes drifted to neck, then to the cleavage she'd exposed. This didn't go unobserved. I reached my sore hand to touch her calf, then ran it gently up to the back of her knee, and stroked at the back of her thigh. Smooth. Warm.

"There are parts of me that don't hurt, you know."

Livia made a slow smile, but she did not move away.

I took the ice pack, letting her hand slide from beneath mine. She straightened as I continued the gentle tickling beneath her blue linen skirt.

"Now why should I be taking care of the parts that aren't injured?" She laughed.

"All of a sudden they want some attention."

"I'll bet," she teased. "Come on then. I guess I'll have to do most of the work. Again."

Holding the sore hand, Livia led me to the bedroom.

She sat on the edge of the bed and leaned back on her elbows. A pose I especially enjoyed. She stared, bright-eyed, with expectation. The tip of her tongue appeared at the corner of her mouth, hungry.

I stepped closer and tried to unbutton my shirt. The heavy gauze bandage wouldn't let me.

"Here. Take it off." I held out my hand.

She undid the thing, none too gently, exposing swollen knuckles.

"That's ugly." She made a face.

"Don't look," I said, fumbling at the buttons.

"I want to look," she said, mischief twisted her grin.

"Do you like to look?" I teased.

Livia shrugged. "Well enough. Probably not as much as most men, but I like it well enough. Do you?"

"Well enough." Again with the tease. "Don't know why." I dropped my shirt on the floor. The slacks followed.

"I know why," Livia said.

"Why?" I asked, dropping the boxers next. My excitement showing.

"Because we look good doing it," she said. Her smile broadened.

"True enough. Ya'll look pretty good when you're done, too."

"So you're one of those boys that like us best when we get down to the altogether, huh?"

It was my turn to shrug. "I like stockings well enough, I guess. But those usually get shucked pretty quick."

Livia giggled. My excitement was full blown and flagging in the wind, so to speak.

I reached out for her hands. I gasped as she got a hold of my injured knuckles. Despite that, I pulled her up. Reaching for the hem of the linen dress, I lifted it over her head.

"The altogether, sir." She took me by the shoulders and changed places. A not too gentle push threw me on my back across the bed.

She walked around to rummage the chest of drawers. God she could walk. It's the hips. Always the hips.

Out came her silk stockings. Livia turned to stand above my head.

The view was up past dark bush, flat belly, jutted breasts, to the smile looking down at me.

She brought up a leg to rest against my shoulder. The one that didn't hurt. Now the view included an expanse of thigh and calf. She bent to draw a stocking over little pink toes, pulling it over her heel, and working it up her leg. Tugging here and there to keep it smooth and straight. Fingers rolled the top down a bit. A quick pinch and twist of the roll, then a tuck back under the stocking.

"Lickety-split, now it won't fall down," Livia said watching my discovery of a little feminine trick.

"Magic." I reached up to touch the silk and the flesh beneath.

The process repeated with the other leg to my great pleasure. Almost as much pleasure as her climbing onto the bed over me. Almost as much pleasure as her mouth finding my aching, stiff member And, maybe, I gave her the same with my mouth, sore jaw and all.

I left Livia to nap, threw on trousers and shirt, to watch out the window. With the rain gone, the sun came out and Galveston became a steam bath. With all the care of a cat burglar, I raised all the closed windows, wincing at every creak and squeal. All except those in the bedroom. A breath of wind seeped in but helped little.

Livia was on my mind as I watched. We needed to talk about the night in the Handmaiden's garden. She'd been dodgy about it. What did she know? Something had to help.

Before long, Livia came out to stand beside me. In the light of the window she glowed with a gentle sheen. Some of her curls clung to her temple.

"Too hot," she said, eyes bleary and wrinkled sheets left impressions on her cheek and shoulder.

"Want coffee?"

"Lord, no," she answered. "Some Irish on ice, maybe?"

I gave her a nod and left for the ice box. The clinking of ice in the glasses made a serenade when I brought them back. Livia took hers to press it to her jaw before taking a sip.

"Any left for you to get some for your face?"

"Had enough of that for now. I'll kill the pain with the Irish."

Livia smiled and nodded. "Might be a good choice."

We kept close to the window, catching whatever breeze that managed to reach us. Watching. A car clattered by every now and then. Porky and a handful of neighborhood kids chased each other back and forth with a lot of noise and laughter. Another boy, his bike laden with sacks, pedaled by throwing the afternoon paper.

I pasted a thoughtful frown on my face. Hoping it appeared intent and worrisome. Hoping she would notice before my cheeks ached from the effort.

Her glass was near empty when she turned. "Wee, that don't look good. What's the matter?"

I shrugged and sipped. "Nah. Nothing really. Just trying to puzzle it all out."

"Stumped good, huh?"

"Sure."

"I wish I could help."

"You might could help," I said.

"How?"

"Give me what you know about the night Godines died. Any detail you can remember. Something might help. Please?" I asked, careful not to bring it in too close, not to seem real personal.

Livia gave me a stare. Maybe there was fear there. A struggle. She sighed, resigned to it maybe. "All right. What do you want to know?"

"What did you see? Hear? Who was there? In the garden that night, I mean?"

She let out a breath. "I didn't... We..." Livia started. "My fella and I went out back."

"Fella?"

"My customer. My john, for God's sake. Really, Conner."

"Sorry. I am. You don't tell what you don't want to tell."

"I was busy with making sure he enjoyed himself. That's what I paid attention to. We heard a thrashing sound. Like somebody falling into the hedge." She shook her head. "It's a sound I heard before. It's not uncommon where I work."

Livia slugged me on the arm. "Don't laugh."

"I didn't."

"You started to."

"Again, I'm sorry. I'll be good."

"We... He cinched up and we went around the corner. My... The man was lying there. My fella left. Ran right out the gate. Left me standing there."

I waited for more. Livia stared out the window.

"Anyone else out there?"

"Dolly was. Her and another gentleman. Around the side of the house, I think. I guess they heard the noise. Anyway, she was the one that screamed. Her fella ran in to get Mary."

"Did Dolly see anything?"

"The body. They came in behind me. I think they took a little longer to put themselves together."

That was another picture unforgettable. I thought it over. Livia might have been holding something back. Maybe I wanted her to be. To have some answers that might help. Answers I could pry out of her somehow.

"Did you hear that?" Livia asked.

"What?"

"I think someone's knocking at your back door."

I heard it then. Light enough tapping, unmistakable. Don't know why the sound got my stomach knotted up, but it did.

With a nod, I sent Livia to the bedroom and fished my – Maceo's – pistol from its drawer. Tip-toeing did not keep the floorboards quiet and every creak and squeal got the cringing regret it deserved.

I squatted in front of the oven and away from the back door.

"Yeah?"

"It's me. Bobbie Lee. Come on. I gotta get in. I'm by myself."

The door got opened but I looked past Bobbie Lee just in case. Nothing but empty yard and trees in the sunlight.

"The back door?" I asked.

"I think we got trouble, Conner. There are people watching the house."

THE JUNKIE

"Jesus Christ, they found me!" Livia had disobeyed me and stood at the kitchen door.

"What the hell, Bobbie Lee?" I asked as I shot a look of disapproval at Livia.

"There's two men watching the house. Down the street. I saw 'em," he said.

I pushed past Livia, and her defiant eyes, to go to the front windows. There was nothing to see. The couple of cars parked across the street were familiar. And empty. Porky, my young lookout, and his friends played sword fight in the muddy shade.

"Where?"

"Off to the right. In front of that yellow house with the iron fence."

Couldn't see them. Too great an angle.

"Coming up Market. I stopped to let this Ford cross," Bobbie Lee said. "Two men inside. I recognized one of them."

"Who?"

"That hophead from town. Always hanging around the Strand in that dirty white suit. Glasses. Glassy. Something."

"Yeah. I kind of remember him. Something Di Glassi. Had a reputation," I said.

"For what?" Livia asked, eyes worried.

"For doing just about anything for money," Bobbie Lee said. He could have left that unsaid.

"They're watching the house? This house? You're sure?" I asked.

"I'm sure." Bobbie Lee nodded. "I circled the block. They stared so hard at your place they didn't give me a glance."

"After that?"

"I just pulled in next door, came around, and knocked." He bobbed his fist as if to repeat the gentle tapping Livia heard. "I hoped they didn't recognize the car."

"Me, too." My heartfelt thought.

Livia grabbed my forearm, eyes desperate. "I can shoot. Give me a gun."

I chuckled. "I'm figuring it'll be a bad day for those two with you packing. I'll see to it. But you never know where bullets go once they start bouncing around. Don't want that here. So I think we'll run."

"I like that idea, me," Bobbie Lee said. "Now sounds like a good time."

It didn't take much to fish out my own pistol from its place in the drawer.

"Get something to carry this thing." I handed the short barreled, ugly Colt .38 to Livia but didn't let go when she grasped it. I meant what I said. That was a belly gun, made for close up killing. If she cut loose with that no telling what got hit. "This is just for you. Don't go using it unless you have to. And make sure you're right up close to 'em," I warned. Livia nodded.

Bobbie Lee handed me the key to the Studebaker.

"Livia, you climb in the front and crouch down on the floor," he said to her as she stuffed my pistol into the bag she got.

"I'm not afraid of them, Bobbie Lee."

"Yes you are," I told her. "And good. You need to be. We are. Do what he says. We're supposed to protect you."

She gazed at me a moment before she nodded.

"Bobbie Lee, go first but get in last. Eyes opened. When that engine turns over, we're stopping for nothing."

And we didn't.

Down the stairs and across the back yard. Bobbie Lee near crashed into the Negro man from the car. A good Texan, he was fast to pull his .38 Police Special. The man's eyes grew big as silver dollars. He turned and fled toward the front of the house screaming. "They're running! They're running!"

Bobbie Lee charged to the other side of the car, taking cover at the rear wheel. Livia rounded him to climb in the front. Dutifully, she ducked to the floor.

The Studebaker turned over instantly, thank God. I ground the gears into reverse and stomped the accelerator, barely giving Bobbie Lee a chance to jump onto the running board.

The Studebaker's inline six cylinders went from sputter to growl, spinning down the neighbor's drive. The youngish Negro half-turned to eye us over his shoulder. Just beyond him, Di Glassi, the hophead, reached into his seedy white suit and pulled out a real big pistol. I watched his slack-jawed surprise turn to angry scowl. He moved toward the street as if to cut us off.

A good choice. That way led toward Broadway. Toward all the best paths to escape. The way I wanted to go.

The hophead aimed his pistol. The engine growl went to howl, screaming backwards up the street. Away from Broadway.

"Shit! Go! Go! Go!" Bobbie Lee pounded the canvas roof.

Front window, two men running toward us.

Back window, a Nash barely missed.

Front window, a hophead pointing his pistol.

Back window, over-steering sent the Studebaker toward a Norfolk pine.

Front window, the two thugs still coming.

Back window, a cross street.

Thank God.

A quick jerk of the steering wheel backed us into it but the car almost flipped over. I braked, but easily, and hoped I wouldn't send Bobbie Lee clean off the thing. He climbed into the back seat, face flushed and grinning. "Well, that was fun," he said.

Livia looked up at me with wide, accusing eyes. "Where are they?"

"Down the block," Bobbie Lee answered for me. "They stopped running when we turned off."

"Are we gonna just sit here?" Livia asked as she squirmed up to sit properly in the seat. Her eyes never left mine.

"Are we?" Bobbie Lee peered out the open window.

I had to take a breath before easing the Studebaker forward, not grinding the gears this time, to stop in the dead center of the intersection. Down a couple of blocks, the two men stood in the middle of the street staring at us. Di Glassi turned and started running away from us. The other man followed.

Bobby Lee realized it first. "Christ! They're going to get their car."

"Maybe we should leave. Do you think?" Livia said.

"I think," I agreed.

Four blocks later, they were there, stopped in the crossroad. I cursed silently. Same at the next one. I could make out Di Glassi's pale face staring out the Ford's open window.

We made a cat and mouse ballet, him always between me and Broadway. As he watched, I screamed a U-turn and raced back the other way. Three blocks later, at the street I picked to turn, the Ford sat blocking the way. Again my foot slammed down on the accelerator.

"Dammit!"

"This can't go on, man," Bobbie Lee said.

True. Half a block down, I braked to a stop. "I'll head toward Seawall. Fool him. Maybe."

Possibly I did. He was not back at the previous cross street, so I hooked a left and headed for the Gulf as fast as could be done.

Except for the old lady I had to dodge. Except for the moving van trying to back into a driveway and blocking the entire street. I hoped to be forgiven the heavily fragrant Sweet Olive tree I destroyed and the lawn I rutted. The moving van? I don't think its crew forgave all the sand and gravel the Studebaker threw at it. Their shrill curses and obscene gestures followed us until I couldn't see them anymore.

The car skidded left onto Seawall Boulevard. Before I could get it stopped. Somebody got rear-ended trying to avoid hitting us.

Before I could bless my luck for being alive, Di Glassi's Ford piled onto Seawall Boulevard. In a cloud of burning rubber not six blocks up the road.

My U-turn took the entire width of Seawall. Vacationers' vehicles and local delivery trucks skidded and scattered in every direction. The drivers' curses could not be heard over the Studebaker's engine, but the tenor bleats of the car horns could.

The muddle of traffic slowed Di Glassi and we gained some distance between us and them. Gave me a chance to catch a breath. A chance for Livia, frightened to her bones, to accuse me of a great wrong with her eyes.

"You all right?" I asked. She just kept that razor glare. "Sorry."

"Damn, Conner. Damn."

"I'm with her. Didn't expect you'd be the one to kill me today." Bobbie Lee shifted to hang out of the window, disgusted with my driving.

"Well, the day's young," I yelled back at him.

Not so young actually. At first, I thought it looked like rain. But, as we fled past Fort Crockett, the sun had settled behind the bank of clouds that had scared Livia earlier that day.

Soon thereafter, too soon, the paved road petered out. Crushed shell replaced pavement. The wheels ground their way over it, slowing our pace.

The Ford grew larger in the rearview mirror. Not good. The damned rain-damped shell prevented any dust trail to conceal us. And night was too slow coming.

For no reason I could name, I noticed my jaw muscles ached from clenching tight. I forced them to relax. That hurt even more. Things were desperate. We'd run out of road before long. Hell, we'd run out of island.

"Damn. Damn. Damn," I spat.

"We got to do something, Conner." Bobbie Lee realized the same thing I did.

"I know. I know." Something. But I didn't know what.

My eyes searched the dunes and grasses. The white and yellow dots of late Spring flowers. Here and there, spaces between the dunes showed peeks of the Gulf, restless and dark with the coming night. More rare, small roads cut the dunes to make a way to the Gulf or snaked toward the Bay for fishermen. These gave me a shadow of a plan. A suicide more like, but still a plan.

"Bobbie Lee?" I glanced. He sat, facing back, watching Di Glassi.

"Yeah."

"Remember being ambushed?" We were once waylaid up in the woods, in the night, near the Arkansas border. A gang out of Kansas City wanted our load of corn liquor. I killed a man that night. An accident more than a murder. Still vivid these two years since.

"Yeah," he answered.

"Remember what mistake they made?"

"I do."

"If I can help it, I'm not making that mistake. You?"

"I think you got the right of it," Bobbie Lee agreed. I caught his determined nod in the mirror.

"What mistake?" Livia twisted in the seat. She was gray with fear. "What mistake, dammit?

Bobbie Lee, always irrepressible, laughed. "They didn't shoot us."

Those bastards should have. They were gone, not to return, and we had kept our booze.

I took the next little track headed toward the Bay and prayed the sand was firm enough to get me just a short way in. As soon as I saw the Ford turn in behind us, I pounced on the brake, and plowed grit to a stop.

The Ford halted some fifty paces short of the Studebaker. Di Glassi and his friend watched us out of the windshield as if unsure of us. That changed when Bobbie Lee and I piled out of opposite sides of the car. For all that chasing, they tried to turn around. To flee?

A mistake. The Ford quickly bogged down in the softer sand.

Maceo's big Colt remained down at my side. All my tough thoughts had me erupting out of the car, gun blazing like some cowboy in the Western movies. There, in the reddish glow of dusk, I guessed I wasn't really that kind of a guy. Find out what they wanted. Like I didn't know. Give them a chance. Like they deserved one. Pure yellow hesitation.

Didn't matter. Di Glassi made my decision when he and his partner exploded from the Ford, their guns blazing.

That stopped me short. Di Glassi held a small automatic and he unloaded it in my direction. The bullets from his little pistol went everywhere but to what he meant to hit. So far, anyway. Luck of the Irish.

I raised the Colt. Old school, because I learned to shoot a pistol with my old man's single action, I pulled the hammer back, leveled it, and lined up the sights on the largest part of Di Glassi I could find. A quick squeeze, a flash, and a roar slapping my face. Di Glassi jerked up stiff and fell over backwards. Against his Ford.

For the first time, I noticed the silence. Bobbie Lee stood on the other side of the car looking down. I knew without seeing that he pointed his own pistol at the Negro laid out on the sand.

"Bobbie Lee?"

"Mine's dead," he answered without turning.

My stomach rolled as I approached Di Glassi. He was still alive, legs out and shoulders propped against the running board. A big bloody spot spread across his chest. I saw the little automatic still in his hand.

"Damn you," he gurgled and took a gasp. "Damn you."

Blood drooled from the corner of his mouth.

I had to cough to unstick the catch in my throat. "Who sent you? Who wants you to kill Livia?"

Di Glassi's eyelids flickered and he tried to focus on me. Another struggling breath.

"Who the hell's Livia?" His eyes rolled and a last bubbling breath escaped. I had killed my second man.

The world spun in the opposite direction of my stomach. Knees no longer wanted to work. Livia's sob snapped me back. Brought some bit of strength to me.

She stood, trembling, by the Studebaker, staring at the man sprawled in the sand, that stupid pistol tight in her hand.

I managed to come up to her, the crushed shell crunching loudly in the twilight. Reaching gently, I pulled the pistol from her hand. She stiffened as I put an arm around her, like she didn't want to be touched. Livia opened her mouth a couple of times before she could manage to talk.

"I'd a' shot 'em if they killed you," she said finally leaning against me.

THE DAMN RANGERS

"That's what he said?" Manny asked, looking down at Di Glassi's body.

"With his dying breath," I answered.

"Exact words?"

"Yep." I looked away. Up at the thumbnail moon, bright above the shadowy, grassy sand.

"And you don't think he came out to whack Livia?"

"No, I don't."

Manny cocked over on one hip and slid a hand in his pocket. I watched the breeze flick at his dark hair across a forehead that shone pale in the moonlight. He let out a breath. "I'll be checking on that. If there's a contract out on you..."

I didn't like the sound of that. Not one bit. Who'd want to hurt little ol' me? A sweet, innocent babe in this world of pain.

"What the hell did I do?"

Manny's lips twisted into a wry smile. "I got a better question. Who you did it to?"

I spat out a gross obscenity. Manny chuckled.

"I will. Thank you. Your mother and your sister," he said.

"Sister might be nice enough. Mom'll give you the clap though." I cracked a smile of my own. Manny laughed out loud.

"You even have a sister?" he asked.

I shook my head.

"You're a good boy, Conner. Best Paddy on the Island. Feel better?"

"Yeah, I do." That surprised me. "Did you see Livia?"

I had made her ride in with Bobbie Lee when I sent him to get Manny. An hour ago, or so.

"A passin' glance."

"And?"

"Tough as my Granna's chuck steak, that one."

"Glad to hear it. She was pretty shook up, last I saw her," I said, relieved. "Did Bobbie Lee get her to the Handmaiden?"

"They were on their way, last I saw 'em."

I made a gesture toward the bodies by the Ford. "What are we going to do?"

As I said it, we saw headlights coming from town. Two cars sandwiching a truck. Manny eyed them, intent, suspicious.

They went on past. I saw the shield embossed on the side of the lead car.

"Sheriff," I said.

"That's the damn Rangers." Manny let out his own obscenity. "Shit."

I thought we were clear, but the damn things came to a halt about a block down.

"They spotted my truck," Manny said as the little caravan began to back up. He looked around, wild-eyed. "All right. All right. Those bastards get to the track, I'm laying down some rounds. Hold 'em up for a bit. I hope. When I do, you head for that bog. Get in the reeds."

A quick look showed them about forty, fifty odd paces off. "I'll do it."

"Keep my truck between the Rangers and you, if you can. I'll be right behind you, I guarantee."

Well, I told myself I'd try, but once more in that endless night, I wasn't all that sure my knees'd carry me.

The Rangers and their friends stopped where our track met the shell road. Manny pulled the long, heavy pistol he carried in his belt. "Ready?"

I nodded.

A man stepped out of the Ranger car, a big white cowboy hat set straight on his head. Another, hatless and in a suit as pale as Di Glassi's, followed him out.

Manny crouched low and stepped behind the Ford. As more men emerged from the caravan, he pointed his pistol toward the road. I noted he aimed low. And maybe a bit to the right. He fired twice, quickly. Waited. Then twice more.

I didn't wait. I bent even lower than Manny to chug my way into the reeds. Ankle deep muck tried to suck my shoes right off my feet.

God, it stank to high heaven of corruption and dead things.

Manny popped the rest of his ammunition into the night. I heard panicked shouting from the road then the eruption of return fire cracked. At least one round hissed through the reeds, snapping loose one or two of them. My neck crunched down like a turtle ducking into its shell.

I heard Manny's shoes slapping sand right before he piled onto me, dumping us both into the reeking muck. He crabbed over and beyond me on all fours, squirming deeper into the bog.

Rolling over took great effort and making a way after him seemed more slither than crawl. Soon enough we huddled together in the shadows.

Manny panted in heavy gasps. "Maybe – maybe that'll do."

"You – get – any of them?"

It took him a minute of struggle to talk again.

"Hell no. And I didn't try." He saw the look in my eye. "I ain't stupid enough to shoot no damn Ranger."

"Rangers. Christ. They're after me too?" I said.

"Maybe," Manny said. He raised up a bit to peer through the

reeds. Another clatter of gunfire. He ducked as some bullets clipped at the reeds above us. "Maybe not."

"No?"

"Could be somebody heard all your shootin'. Could be they were just out looking for boats bringing in some liquor."

"Let's hope that's true," I said. "Better lam it. Those bastards move someone back up the road, they can cut us the hell off. Trap us in this stink hole."

"Best thing you've said since warning me off your mother."

Sorry Momma, it was a joke. We slopped deeper into the reeds. Another volley of shots flew. Some thumped hard into metal. The truck, I guessed. Some sheared more reeds. A couple hissed over our heads. Got that turtle duck again.

Half an eternity passed feeling that stinking sludge squishing between my fingers, stopping to retrieve mud-stolen shoes, and soaking up oily slime before we found the edge of the reeds.

I stared and I listened. Scruffy, assorted grasses, almost black in the night, breathed back and forth in the wind. Here and there a stray bush stuck up as if defying nature. And, God help us, clumps of prickly pear cactus dared anyone to wander across the prairie-like stretch of firm land. Off in the distance a few fisherman's shacks stood on their stilts. Behind everything, the lights of Fort Crocket and Galveston glowed in the sky. If someone guarded our exit, I couldn't see them.

"How long before dawn, do you think?" I asked.

Manny's eyes darted back and forth as we knelt in the edge of filth and cane. "An hour or two, I guess. I pray."

"We need to get this crap cleaned off of us if we can." I hadn't noticed before, but my arms and hands, hell, my face too, were covered with shallow slashes. Torn by the razor edges of the reeds.

"Yeah. Think we can cross the road? Get to the beach?"

"Don't you think the Bay's closer?"

"Maybe. But it's near as filthy as this bog. At least out here." Manny shook his head.

"Let's go."

When the sand firmed, the reeds ended. We stayed as close as we could to them and moved, in a crouch, toward the road. Stopped in the shadow.

More looking and listening.

"What do you think?" Manny asked.

"Looks quiet enough." I shrugged. "One at a time to cover each other? Just in case. Or both together and the hell with it?"

"The hell with it. If we're seen – well, too damn bad for us," Manny said.

I could have used a bit more encouragement. We took one last look around.

"Go," Manny hissed.

We sprinted across the grass. Crunched over the crushed shell road. Swished through the tangle of vines that covered the dunes. Slapped over the packed sand of the beach.

Manny and I both, winded and panting, squealed like girls when we halted. We made it. We were alive.

Maybe, anyway. Manny eased back part way up a dune to take a look. A long look.

I drug up a stray piece of lumber, put my money on it then laid my pistol on the bills. Then, shoes, clothes, and all, I went to get a thrashing in the surf.

The removal of the sticky, reeking muck was a tangible thing. I felt it leave my body in the tepid churn. When I stood in the water, sometimes thigh deep – sometimes chest deep, the waves pounded and shoved at me.

Manny was near me now. He laughed. He fought the surf. Each wave that broke against him a victory.

Finally, he surrendered to the Gulf, letting one wave knock him back a couple of feet.

"We need to go," he said. I looked shoreward as if there was a reason to run. "Dawn's coming. We probably need to be far from here by daylight."

A good enough reason to me.

Out of the water, my soaked shoes became a burden. As soon as my money and pistol got tucked away, they came off. We hoofed down the beach, shoes dangling in our hands. Mile after mile. At first, my wet shirt clung to me, a second skin and chilly in the breeze. An hour later, we were mostly dry, though the dried salt made our clothes stiff. The sun had risen from the Gulf.

It still took us to midday to make it to Murdoch's Bathhouse. Feet sore, clothes stained, eyes swollen. Exhausted. Thirsty. Starved.

One of Manny's crew drove me to an empty flat. I fell asleep in a soapy tub. And again on the couch, naked and covered in a sheet.

When I awoke, close to dusk, I found out that I had gotten away with murder.

Pounding on my door woke me. The upstairs door. Scared the hell out of me. Where was Porky?

I drew up my sheet tight over my shoulders and shuffled to the door. There stood Bobbie Lee, fist pulled back, ready to pound some more. A concerned Livia looked at me, dark eyes wide.

"Well finally." Bobbie Lee said. "I was about to kick it in,"

"Where the blazes is Porky?" I grunted, my heart still throbbing in my throat.

"I sent him home," Livia said, raising up on tip toe to peer over Bobbie Lee's shoulder. "He's got no business here if people are gonna be shooting, dammit."

"Anyway, he was knocking and knocking." Bobbie Lee said. "Couldn't get nothin' out of you. I been making a wreck outta your door for a while. You didn't hear?"

I shook my head, but I opened the door enough to let them in.

"Get some clothes on," Livia said as she brushed by me.

I did that for her. Sort of. When I plopped down with them in the kitchen, Livia reached over, unbuttoned the three buttons I managed, tugged the shirt straight, and buttoned it up proper.

"Didn't find an A-shirt to throw on under that?" she asked.

"Forgot."

Livia shook her head like women do when they show disapproval to men.

Bobbie Lee, in his turn, broke out in a big boyish grin.

"What?"

"You, sir, are the luckiest Paddy in the whole damned world," he proclaimed.

I cocked an eyebrow at him as he reached into a canvas bag I hadn't noticed before. He slapped a newspaper down on the table, then leaned back, crossed arms, and stared at me.

My eyes stared back until Livia nudged me.

"Read," she commanded.

I flopped it over.

The glaring headlines said that this year's Bathing Beauty event opened today. And, in case anyone doubted it, several photographs of young women in beach wear smiled across their shoulders at me.

Up came my hand and my bewilderment. I repeated, "What?"

Livia poked a finger at another headline and puffed her exasperation. "Can you read, or do you want me to read it to you?"

"Gun Fight on the West End," I read. But the line beneath got me sitting up. "Rangers Slay Two Bootleggers."

"Rangers slay two bootleggers," Bobbie Lee whistled. "We are off the hook."

"Well aren't those Rangers prize Rangers," I had to admit. "They can come and sit by me in hell."

"Those your plans for the future? Sitting in hell, I mean?" Livia asked.

I smiled. "Not my immediate plans."

As if on their own, my fingers started drumming a tattoo on the table top. My insides stormed. That was not helped by the newspaper, though I guessed it should have.

"What's the matter?" Bobbie Lee asked.

"Don't know. I'm angry. Some circus freak tried to assassinate us.

I had to kill someone. The Handmaiden's mess is still a mess." I stood up, paced the kitchen, sat down. Stood up again. They stared at me, Bobbie Lee worried, Livia amused. I glared. "Be right back."

When I returned, I carried the Colt and my cleaning kit. The pistol was a disaster but one I could do something about. I put it on the table and started disassembling it.

"Well, at least he's not gonna shoot us with it," Bobbie Lee said to Livia. She nodded.

"Cook up some breakfast, Bobbie Lee." It was not a request.

He made eggs and ham. Aggrieved but he did it. I brushed, wiped, and oiled. Livia, after several moments of working me over with her eyes, read the paper.

"Holy Jesus Christ and his muddy sandals!" Livia exploded. She shoved the newspaper under my nose.

The article, buried back on page four, said that Di Glassi, one of the slain bootleggers, was suspected of the murder of Peter Godines.

"How 'bout that, Conner?" Livia asked.

The story stunned me. "I don't believe he did it."

"Of course he didn't."

"I don't get it." I whispered.

"Of course you don't. But the cops gave you a gift. They found an easy way to close a case, so they took it. They gave you a wide open door."

"So what happens if I find out who really did do it?"

"When you find who did it," Bobbie Lee reminded me.

"Right. Right. When I do," I rushed to agree. Folks had expectations, and they suddenly weighed that much heavier. "What's the Law gonna do? They think they got their killer."

"It's all right, Conner. The Handmaiden – or Mary – will be the one dealing with it in the end. Not the damned Law," Livia said.

That was an ugly fact brought home to roost. My job was to bring Godines' killer to the Handmaiden, not to the law. And, God help whoever that was. I nodded.

Bobbie Lee brought over plates of breakfast, then glasses of warm, flat beer from a pail that had been sitting in the ice box. "Then go find 'im."

Livia took a tentative sniff. "You gotta get one of those refrigerators. Everything's always cold."

The comment wasn't helping my mood. I shot her a look.

"Didn't mean nothing, Conner. Just talking to talk. Swear." Why did I find some of her apologies lined with challenges?

I let out a breath and made a pressing motion with my palm. "The crap had to be put somewhere in the back of my brain. Get Godines back on the front burner. The hell with folks shooting at me. The hell with being so angry."

"You bet," Livia said, still with an air of challenge.

"Thinking on it, I figure there's no more people wanting Godines dead," I offered.

"I sure can't think of nobody else," Bobbie Lee said.

"Me either," Livia put in.

Couldn't help giving her a glance. She was on my list still. Did she know?

"So," I said. "We are pretty sure who wanted him dead. Let's find out who had the chance to make him dead."

"Don't follow," Bobbie Lee said, hands in the air inviting explanation.

"We gotta find out where all these people were on that night, at that hour," I explained.

"Who doesn't have an alibi? You are so long winded sometimes," Livia chided.

"I'm Irish. We do that." I didn't look at Livia. Did she notice?

"However you say it, Conner," Bobbie Lee said. "We can't ask those folks. Not after the way we riled 'em."

That was true enough. I thought a minute. "There's one I figure we can still ask. Whether we'll get an answer, I can't say."

"Who?" they both said.

"Chief Higgins."

"Why?" again in unison.

"Because one of those guys that came after us was a Negro." I took a glance out the window at the late afternoon sun. "We'll go in the morning."

Sounded easy enough, but like most easy things, it just got harder.

Next morning. Early. Somebody woke me banging a hammer on my wall. I threw on pants as Livia, pressing the sheet tight across her breasts, stared at me with frightened eyes.

Maceo's pistol and I went down the stairs to find Manny Dents and his pistol rapping the door frame. One of his crew stood behind him and watched the street. Manny didn't wait for me to ask him what the hell he was doing here.

"Get your stuff. They hit Papa last night. We're going to the mattresses."

"Shit." Not Papa. Because of me?

"You and Livia come with me. Tell Bobbie Lee to get your car to the garage across the street from The Palace Hotel. Let's go."

THE PALACE

The Palace Hotel and Gulf Side Resort took up most of the block between 22nd and 23rd, two streets inland from Seawall Boulevard. A series of square, sun-bleached and salt-worn, stucco buildings that were once apartments. That's what it looked like anyway.

Between each building sat rough cabanas with brown palm fronds that shaded collections of cast iron benches, chairs, and tables.

Under the portico of the western-most building, two hard-eyed characters sat on worn chaise lounges of wicker and bamboo, sipping an iced drink and pretending to read newspapers. As Manny led Livia and me up to them, one dropped his section of the paper to the ground. The working end of a big, double-barreled shotgun poked from beneath the pages.

Manny shook his head at the man and bent to pull the paper over the thing. The man cocked his head in apology.

Inside I found a dark hallway, lit by a row of bare bulbs on the ceiling, and a single stairway to the right.

"We're upstairs. Livia gets a room in the back. We get the rest," Manny said as he started up the stairs.

"We?" I asked.

"Me and my crew. You and your partner. If he gets here. Some other boys. A couple of other crews already got the downstairs. Fifteen guys, maybe."

At the top of the stairs, dark and also dimly lit with bare bulbs, Manny took us to the far room. An all-in-one with a kitchenette along the back wall and a small window over the tiny sink. A well-used, drab couch and chair crowded the right side of the room. A Murphy Bed filled half the left wall. Beside that a small chest of drawers sat beneath a window.

"Hey, look. That's one of those refrigerators," Livia said. She walked through the room, dumping my cardboard suitcase on the couch. She opened cabinets to find stoneware and glasses. Flatware lay in a single drawer to the right of the sink. "Delightful."

"We stuck some food in the ice box," Manny said.

"Refrigerator," she corrected.

"Whatever. You may have to do some cooking for the boys."

"Ha. The boys are gonna be disappointed," she laughed. I nodded. Livia did better with bandages than with supper.

"Toilet and shower are across the hall. You'll be sharing," Manny said.

"There's a lock on the door, right?" Livia asked, eyes full of alarm.

"There's a lock." Manny told her. Then to me. "Bring your stuff."

My stuff was a pillow case crammed with some clothes and toiletries. My room, directly street side of Livia's, was empty except for three men from Manny's crew, a stack of cotton-stuffed mattresses, and the kitchenette.

"Carlo," Manny said as we stepped inside. "Throw a couple of mattresses over by the door." Then to me. "For you and your partner. Throw your stuff there against the wall. I know you want to talk."

I did. Manny let me follow him back outside. He hustled up a couple of those iced drinks for us. Acidic, over-sugared, lemonade, over-weighted with something alcoholic.

Well, no one showed signs of going blind from it.

We took our drinks to one of the cabanas. This one sorely needed some extra palm fronds, but there was shade enough and a breeze. A couple of cushions for the cast iron chairs would've been nice.

"What's with all the cars?" I asked. They were bumper to bumper and parked along the street. Couldn't all be ours.

"The Bathing Beauty Parade's today, remember?"

"Oh yeah. Forgot."

"Told my crew to stay here. Don't think there's enough guns in all of town to keep 'em off Seawall, though. Stupid bastards."

"No one'd start gunning over there, would they?"

"Doubt it. But no one's keeping the Town guys away from the Parade either." Manny sipped the tart drink.

"What happened to Papa?"

"Don't know for certain. He didn't show up to get with his new boys yesterday. I went over to his place. It was tore up pretty good. He wasn't there."

"Did they kill him?"

"Not there, I don't think. There was a bit of blood scattered here and there. Beat him up pretty good."

"But he was alive when they took him, right?" If anyone knew the signs of a beating – or a shooting – Manny was that one. I waited for him to nod anyway. "So he might be all right?"

"Sorry, Conner. I know he was your friend. They took him for a ride. We won't be seeing him anymore."

"Somebody's days are numbered, goddammit," I managed.

"Actually, Papa's days ended to get back at somebody else's sin," Manny said.

"Good Lord. Who?"

"You."

"Me?"

"You got one of theirs. So they went out and got one of ours. The way of things."

"Di Glassi?"

"He's a Town man." Manny shrugged.

"But, I was defending myself."

Manny shook his head. "Poor Irish sod. You think that matters."

"So we just go to the mattresses and trade off murders for the rest of the year?"

"Something like that. For most of us. At least until Mr. Quinn and Big Jim Clark work it out. I don't think you have that luxury though," Manny said. Quinn bossed the Beach Gang and Big Jim bossed the Town Gang while Johnny Jack Nounes did a stretch in prison.

"Why not me?"

"Because Rose Maceo wants you out finding Godines killer," Manny answered.

"The Town guys gone to the mattresses, too?"

"Yeah. Why?"

"Because there's a contract out on me. That's why. Learn anything more about that?

"Not much," Manny said. "The contract went out before Di Glassi. So it's not about all of this. It's open, so anybody can collect."

"Anybody?" My insides went cold.

"Even me," Manny laughed.

Well, wasn't that the sugar in the pie. My eyes couldn't help drifting to the pistol stuck in Manny's belt.

He laughed again. "Don't worry, Conner. You're my friend. Anybody messing with you messes with me."

"Thanks, Manny." I did feel reassured. Flattered as well. A man like Manny Dents thought me a friend.

A great roar rose up from the direction of the Gulf.

"Ah. The Parade's starting." Manny chugged down his drink and stood. "Wanta go down? Check out the Bathing Beauties?"

I grinned. "The leg show by the seashore."

I would have liked to go down there. Nothing like a good set of legs. Or even sixty pairs of legs. But I declined. Maybe this was a good time to get around town without getting shot at. A good time to go talk to Chief Higgins.

I went looking for Bobbie Lee.

—

LAQ

—

Found him in Livia's room. The two of them stood in front of her chest of drawers where Bobbie Lee had placed my radio. I guessed he didn't rush to flee the flat. He fiddled with the knobs as Livia supervised, with hands on hips. Blips, whistles, and static.

"Gettin' anything on that box?" I asked.

"Not a damn thing," Bobbie Lee said. "Just seeing if we could get it working."

"Nobody radioing this time of day, anyway," Livia added. "Something to do with the sun, I hear."

I had heard that, too. "Bobbie Lee, I wanta go see Chief Higgins. You game?"

Both of them turned to stare at me.

"You think that's safe, Conner?" Livia asked, alarmed.

I grinned at her. "You hear all that noise down to the beach? I figure everybody's there."

"I'm game, if you're sure," Bobbie Lee said.

"He's sure," I felt Manny's breath on my neck as he spoke. Scared me silly.

"Where the – Jesus, man, I thought you went down to the Bathing Beauties," I exclaimed.

"I couldn't very well do that after telling my crew to stay put, now could I." Manny laughed. "I'll just stay here and ogle Livia."

"Go to ogling me and I'll hit you with a stick," Livia said doubling up a fist.

"Ouch. That wouldn't be fun." Manny said. "Don't worry, Conner. I'll keep her safe. And, hell, soon as that parade's over, there'll be fifteen armed men hanging around."

Good enough, I figured. We went for the Studebaker.

"Reassured?" Bobbie Lee asked as I drove out of Abe's Auto Fix-It shop in the gassed-up car.

I nodded. I kept it close that I was pretty sure folks were gunning for me – not for Livia. I didn't think whoever put down Godines was after her. Not any more, if they ever were. Livia, for all I knew, could have done it herself.

"What are we gonna do about Papa?" Bobbie Lee asked. "Somebody's due, you know."

"I know. I plan on collecting. Don't doubt it."

"We'll have to get it done before Quinn makes his peace. Don't think we should be tipping the tureen when things settle down," Bobbie Lee said.

"We'll get ours. Depend on it," I put more confidence in my voice than I really felt. Them that got Papa most likely knew what they were doing. Bad odds for us.

Clouds gathered as we drove and big drops of rain spattered the windshield as we pulled into Higgins shabby office building. I was right glad to clap on my fedora but we trotted up to the door without getting too wet.

That same little guy that had been with Higgins the last time sat at the desk shuffling a big stack of papers. Two men, obviously dockworkers in rough clothes and newsboy caps, stood over him.

"I 'member you," the little man said. "Gi' me a minute."

He made a quick job of sorting out a couple of stacks of paper and handed one each to the two stevedores. "You get these out to the Zilveren Zee. Chop, chop."

"Yah, suh," they said together.

"Quickest, now."

"Yah, suh."

They pulled heavy sou'wester raincoats from wall pegs, tucked the papers inside, under their arms, and charged out into the rain. Rain that had become a roaring deluge.

"Now, gel'men, how may I help you? My name is Laq, by the way," he said, smiling a toothy grin.

"Mr. Laq..." I started.

"Just Laq. French for lake, I think."

"Laq, I want to see the Chief." Polite was always the best to begin.

"I can fix that up. Tomorrow, maybe. The day after for sure." His smile never faded.

"Today, I think." A little less polite.

"Impossible, suh."

"Why?" I asked. Bobbie Lee crowded up beside me.

"He's out to Pier 19. He's gotta inspect the cargo. Certify the loading and trim. Got two ships. He's gotta be there. Sign off on it. It's required."

"It takes all day to do this?" Bobbie Lee asked.

"It takes as long as it takes," Laq said. "Gotta have it done by tide's turn. That's about three thirty, four, tomorrow morning."

"Why does that matter?" I asked.

"Lubber. That's 'cause with all the water in the Bay flowing out, the ships don't have to fight against it. Unner'stan?" Laq beamed at his knowledge.

That sort of made sense. I nodded. Something he said earlier gave me an idea.

"This signing-off bit. A form, right?"

Laq nodded.

"You have copies of these forms?"

"Yessuh. That's my main job. Making those copies." Laq just couldn't douse that smile.

"They're kept here?"

"'Course, suh."

"I need to see these forms," I said.

For the first time that smile faded. "Impossible, suh. Only authorized folk allowed ta see 'um."

"I'm authorized." I lied.

"Who did that?" Laq frowned.

"I did." I took a step forward trying to be as tall as I could. "Now you can be in the way or out of the way. Choose."

Fear came into his eyes. Laq stood there a moment. I could see his knees shaking through his trousers.

"I'm not thinking they pay you for this. Am I right?" I said.

"You'll catch hell for this," Laq said, but he stepped aside.

I was more than glad that the man caved. Kind of trembley myself.

Higgins' cabinets were an unholy mess. Those certifications ended up deep in the middle drawer of the second one I rummaged through. The latest certifications were shoved into the front of the folder. I appreciated that as I pulled out a fist full of papers.

There they were, sure enough. Maybe about ten down. The dates were right. The times were right. Higgins' signature matched. By all I could tell, he'd spent that night on or near two ships at the time Godines died.

I jammed the papers back into the cabinet as I caught movement. Bobbie Lee had pulled his pistol from his belt.

"Well, I'm damned. Here's two hundred greenbacks right in front of me. All I gotta do is squeeze the trigger." Chief Higgins' voice sounded right behind me. Felt like a big icicle pressed my back bone.

"Pull that trigger, fool," Bobbie Lee said. "You'll be dead 'fore he hits the floor, by God."

I managed, somehow, not to flinch. Not to faint dead away.

Before I could move, Laq said. "He's riflin' the files, Chief. Lookin' for where you were."

"Where I was when?" Higgins asked.

"When Godines got whacked, Chief," I said and turned around. Slowly.

"You still thinkin' I killed that slug?" Higgins lowered his Army issue .45 Colt semiautomatic.

"Not anymore," I said, and reached behind me to push the file cabinet closed. "But I am interested to hear how you found out about the contract on me."

"Just by listening. Always pays to know who's gunning for who."

"Who's gunning for me, Chief?"

"No idea." Higgins pushed his Colt into his pants pocket.

Not helpful.

"How does all that work down here?" I asked. "Up home we did our own killing."

"That happens down here, too."

"But not this time. Not with me. Why's that?"

"No idea." Higgins shrugged a shoulder.

Another answer that didn't help. I turned to face him full on. "Then how the hell did you get to hear about it?"

"Heard it from a guy."

"Which guy?"

"A guy, you know." Higgins gave another shrug.

"Who heard it from a guy who heard it from a guy," Bobbie Lee snarled. He still had not put away his pistol.

"Who heard it from another guy," Higgins said. I saw him start to grin but think better of it.

"Tell me this, then," I rubbed at my lower lip with a knuckle. "If somebody gets me, how do they collect?"

"The last time I remember this happening, whoever did it put an ad in the personals. Said something like, 'expect good news soon,' and included a phone number. The next day the mark was found floatin' off East Beach. I expect somebody gave him a call and made some arrangements to pick up the money."

"What if they didn't pay?" Bobbie Lee asked.

"I'll tell you," Higgins started. "If you'll lower that rod."

Bobbie Lee waited for a nod from me, then stuffed his weapon in his belt.

Higgins grinned. "Tell me, Irish, would you forget to pay someone that just got through killin' a person?"

Sounded like the square dope, like it should be one of the commandments.

"Still with that Irish crap?" Bobbie Lee complained.

"Sorry. Can't tell you apart," Higgins said. Then to me. "Listen, Conner, there's not a smoke ankle my side o' town's got any grief over Godines. Their big brothers neither. Treated 'em right. Bought 'em stuff. Straight up guy. I didn't want 'im dead. I didn't make 'im dead. We jake?"

I paused and made myself hold it. Like I considered whether or not he and I were okay.

"We're jake, Chief."

GANGSTERS ARE STUPID

The bathing beauties packed up their accolades, their daring swim suits, their ribbons and sashes, and returned to their real lives. The reporters, the mucky-mucks, and the crowds left with them. To replace them all came pregnant skies and rain.

Novels and moving pictures had it all wrong. A gang war is mostly boredom. After most nights playing poker with Manny and his crew, I tossed and turned on a lumpy mattress, listened to the rain, and pondered the death of Mr. Godines. I sat on Livia's couch watching her and Bobbie Lee dance to my radio's music through the evenings. Then I repeated the process, day following day.

It was also bad for business. Both gangs had members holding private poker games for high rollers. Didn't happen. Ripe targets, and you didn't want to get your players robbed or hurt. Spooked customers stayed away from the speakeasies and casinos. Couldn't collect our cuts anyway. Of course, Manny wasn't cruising the streets with his men. Several brawls broke out and a lot of stuff got tore up. A few jaws broke. Busted knuckles. The coppers had to handle it, so they weren't all that happy.

I was left losing at cards, thrashing on a mattress, or ogling Livia. She didn't hit me with a stick.

One bright spot. I found a way to make a big smile on Bobbie Lee's face. An antique Mexican man on the beach and on the hustle. Sometime in the middle of each rainless night, he built up a big driftwood fire in a vacant stretch of salt grass a few blocks west. He and his equally ancient wife drug two huge cast iron cauldrons from his beat up truck. In them, the couple brewed up stew. One cauldron had a fish stew. One had what I hoped was beef. The old man sold his delicious fare at the exorbitant price of a dollar a pail to anyone who'd show up with their own pail.

The old señora got another dollar and my pail from me for hauling it down to our door.

"Umm-mm, on my momma's sweet smile, this is good," Bobbie Lee sang just before shoving his third spoonful of his second bowl into his mouth.

Livia and I smiled over our first bowl. Neither of us minded that he always got the lion's share.

"More of that beer?" I asked Livia.

"Mumph," Bobbie Lee grunted.

"I guess that means he wants some too," Livia said.

"Mumph," I imitated, grabbing up the three glasses. I returned them full from the refrigerator.

I watched Bobbie Lee wolf down the stew, barely taking the time to chew, and sipped at the beer. For once, it tasted fairly fresh. Maybe it had something to do with Livia's refrigerator being better than my old ice box.

The two of us helped Livia clean up. With the surfaces wiped down and plates soaped and rinsed and stacked in the dishrack, we took more beer to the couch. Bobbie Lee found a station on the radio. Somebody's swing band counted down all the most popular tunes of the week.

Bobbie Lee shuffled a few steps, a hand out, inviting Livia to dance. She shot him a look.

"Well, looks like I'm out of here. Ya'll have fun," he said.

I gave her a stare, raising an eyebrow.

"So? I didn't want to dance," she said and snuggled close. She put an arm around me. Fingers tickled lightly at my neck. "I know, you know."

"Know what?"

"I know you still think I did it. That I killed Peter."

That sat me up quick. I looked hard at her for a moment. She just looked back.

"No. I still think you might have done it. That's different."

"How is that different?" she challenged.

She couldn't see the difference? I could. Clear as day. "It just is."

Livia sighed her exasperation.

"I know Rose Maceo. He asks you to do something, you do it. Always simple with Rose," she said. "So I know you have to do these things. To think these things."

She dodged me. Saying nothing about that night.

"And?" I asked, wanting something about it.

"And I'm not mad at you for thinking I killed somebody."

She dodged again.

"Gee thanks." I said.

"You're welcome," She said, like her forgiveness meant strong stuff.

It probably did.

"Let me help you?" Livia asked.

"Help me do what?"

"Find Peter's killer."

I smiled. I had to. "What if it's you?"

"Then I guess I'll help you find me. I'm fun to find – most times," She teased.

"That's true," I had to admit. She was.

"So, tell me?"

"Tell you what?"

"What you've been puzzling out all night."

I looked at her a moment. What should I tell? How much should I tell? If she had killed Godines, would I be helping her somehow?

"All right," I started. "I'm working on two folks. Neither of them are particularly happy to see me right now. There are things I need to know."

"From what I've seen of gangsters, they don't usually have trouble getting any answers they need," Livia said.

"I ain't there yet. Don't really want to start something that might blow up in my face."

"You mean you don't want to do anything that'd make Rose mad."

"You are as smart as you are good looking."

"Give it over, Conner."

I sighed. "There's this businessman..."

"That guy Ney."

The girl did listen. Remembered.

"He's got some weight here in town," I said.

"So you got to go around him?"

"Yep."

Livia giggled. "Men are stupid. And, there are days I'm thinkin' gangsters are stupider than most."

"All right, how would you go 'round?"

"He's got folks working for him, right?" Livia asked. "Maybe a girl or two?"

I nodded.

"Dime to your dollar, one of those girls knows more about his life than he does."

I nodded again. I thought I knew such a girl.

Livia smiled and poked my chin with a finger.

"You might be as smart as you are good looking, my dumb Conner," she said. "Don't be making her mad at you like you did him. Use some of that Paddy charm."

"I'll try."

"Good. Now, do you have some of that Irish whisky left?"

"Yep."

"Pour us up some." Livia stepped behind a dressing screen she had found from somewhere.

I sat back on the couch, a glass of whisky in each fist, when she stepped from behind the screen. She wore a shirt of mine I didn't know she had, stockings, and nothing else.

THE SKIRT

"Well, do I look hobo enough for you?" Bobbie Lee asked. A faded black coat over a wrinkled shirt. Blousy knickerbockers without stockings. His scuffed work boots. A newsboy cap. He hadn't shaved, but it didn't show. He looked like a street waif. But he did always have a baby face.

"Good enough. How 'bout me?" I wore a tattered suitcoat and tight black pants showing an inch of my socks. I pulled my own newsboy cap down almost to my eyebrows.

"Clowns in the circus, if you ask me," Manny said, coming in. He wore a robe, and his hair dripped water from his shower.

"Thanks."

"Truth needs to get out. You boys got a plan?" Manny asked.

"Watch and not get noticed," Bobbie Lee said.

"Yeah. Move around some. Every hour or two. Try not to get to talking to anyone if you can help it. Especially you, Bobbie Lee. You ain't looking to make new friends."

"Why me, Manny?"

"Cause I know you, Little Bit. You talk to folks. They'll

remember you." Manny turned to me. "Know where ya'll gonna place yourselves?"

"Yeah. I'll be..."

"Stow it. I don't need to know. Just places where ya'll can see all four sides of the block. And get something done. You don't want Mr. Maceo to get impatient."

"Got it." I nodded.

Manny chuckled. "You boys really do look sad. Don't be turning down any charity. Just take the dimes and tell 'em thanks."

"Got it," I repeated with a grimace. Taking charity just wasn't in my blood.

"Don't get yourselves shot," Manny said. "As far as I know, there's still that contract."

"Yeah. Yeah."

It took us a couple of days to find who we were looking for.

Ney's "girl Friday." Bobbie Lee spotted her getting out of a Tin Lizzy early on a rainy day as he huddled under a tree behind Ney's office building. We got her coming and we knew which direction, roughly, she came from.

"Hooo-raahhhh for us. Don't do us a lick of good," Bobbie Lee said, shedding rain water all over the Studebaker.

"Why not?"

"You ain't no cake eater. Not by a stretch. How do you think you can cozy up to that bit of calico with half of her family staring at you from that car?"

Bobbie Lee was right. I've never been much of a lady's man. I get all wormy inside around most of them if I didn't know them.

I sighed. "Got any ideas?"

"Who, me?" Bobbie Lee asked, grabbing at the dash as I turned hard onto Seawall. "Maybe she goes to the clubs. Church on Sundays. Maybe even to Love's church."

"Yeah, maybe we can get all cozy in the pew. Sing hymns together."

"You want to get her attention, singing is the way to do it."

"You got a problem with my singing?"

"No. I like cows with the croup bellowing at me."

"Fornicate yourself." I turned off Seawall into the neighborhood.

Livia came up with the solution that night as we slurped fish stew.

"Here's your answer," she said, pointing a chunk of bread at me.

"What?

"A girl's gotta eat. Maybe she goes out during work."

"She might."

"At least you'll get a shot at meeting her."

"You're good at this. You should be doing it."

Livia grinned large, eyes twinkling. "I might should. Who knows, maybe she'd like me better."

That was a picture, and I took a moment to fill in a few of those details. She read my thoughts.

"Nasty Paddy. Want dessert?" she asked.

I looked around for pie. Didn't see any, but then Livia's bare foot found my shin. Some days I could be thicker than a slab of bacon.

The next morning, Bobbie Lee returned to his nest across from Ney's office, and I found a way to a roof across the street and opposite it. Missed her completely then and the next day.

Irishman's luck, the rain quit a little after noon. Another good roll of the dice brought her out of the building and walking toward downtown at five minutes after one. I eased back from the ledge just in case she bird watched or something.

To be sure, I kept a lookout from the rooftop for two more days. Like a clockwork toy, those swaying hips strolled from her workplace at three minutes after one.

Skipped the rest of the week. Didn't want the skirt seeing either of us. And I certainly didn't want to be seen by whoever might be gunning for me.

Monday rolled around to find me in my freshly pressed suit, buffed shoes, and dusted fedora. I also reeked of a dose of Manny's White Rose Toilet Water.

"So, hobo enough for ya'll?" I asked. Manny, Bobbie Lee, and Livia stood around giving me a once over.

"Gnat's whistle, Conner," Bobbie Lee assured.

"Swell," Livia said smiling.

"You doll-up real good, Irish. I gotta admit," said Manny.

"Got some scratch?" Bobbie Lee asked.

I patted the roll of bills in my pants pocket. "Enough, I think."

"Have a mop?" Livia asked, putting a couple of fingers down my front jacket pocket.

I'd put the handkerchief in the jacket's side pocket. I double checked with a touch and nodded.

"I gotta earful." The attention was starting to grate. "I'm not gettin' baptized or married, for God's sake."

"But you are," Manny said. "Strolling out in front of three dangerous things."

"Yeah, what are those?"

"A fat cat with a temper, gunmen hunting you, and a skirt."

Livia laughed. "The skirt's the most dangerous."

I had to chuckle at that.

"Well, I do know one dangerous skirt." I said, eyeing her.

She flushed. Maybe she remembered that I still suspected her of killing Godines.

"Don't doubt it, Paddy," she retorted.

"You're right, Conner, enough. Let's batten down a bit and get serious," Manny said.

"I wait on your wisdom, oh honored one," I said.

"Go ahead. Give me some more. Crack wise." All mirth, all kindness, all warmth left Manny's eyes.

"Sorry."

"You're not working a tat on the skirt. Talk to her. You're not a cop. So don't pump. Talk to her. And, when you're done, thank her and leave. Get the hell back here. Yeah?"

"Yeah." I agreed.

"When you're not with her, try to find a way to keep your head down and your eyes opened. Don't be coming home carrying bullets in your back." Bobbie Lee warned.

I'd certainly try to do that. My belly went chill.

"We're gonna worry about you, Conner." Livia said.

I appreciated the sincerity on her face.

"Thanks," I said to all of them. The morning was passing fast. "I gotta wiggle."

"Don't forget to duck," Bobbie Lee said as I opened Livia's door.

"Promise." I pulled the door closed behind me.

Yeah. Duck a bullet? I could've done that. Twice if I needed to. But apple sauce some skirt? I'd get all balled up. Trip over my own tongue.

The drive downtown took forever. Got lucky with parking the Studebaker, however. Across the street from Ney's building, with two cars in front of me, and on the same side that the girl walked down. I could just see the exit if I hunched low and peered through the car windows ahead of me.

Must have been a couple of minutes past one because the girl headed out for her lunch. I followed. Easy, as she was tricked out in pale tan. Pale tan linen cloche hat that showed off bouncy, dark ginger curls. Pale tan linen outfit, low-hung blouse, with wide-cuffed long sleeves. The blouse helped the knee-length pale-tan linen skirt stress the curve of her hips. Tan stockings and tan shoes.

Following her was a pleasant thing. On my Momma's sweet cornbread, that skirt could walk. If poetry could climb off the page and move, that's the way it would do it.

All I needed was a plan. None came to mind. I kept my eyes down, or tried to. Didn't want her to sense being watched. Didn't want being marked for paying too much attention to a pretty girl.

Of course, I had an accident. Bumped into some suit late getting back to work.

"Oh, sorry," I said, not too loud, as we both got turned sideways.

"Watch it, boy." The fortyish businessman straightened his hat.

"Excuse me. Wasn't watching."

The man made a face, turned, and walked off.

It dawned on me, as I hurried to close on the girl, that an accident was a good plan. So I hoped I was unnoticed, and I hoped she'd keep eyes front and head downtown.

I caught up and went to pass her. We bumped. A nice "happy accident."

Took a couple of steps on past her and threw an "excuse me" over my shoulder. Then I did a slight pause to turn to her. She had stopped, startled. An unhappy face.

"I know you," I said. "You work with that shipping guy, Ney. Mr. Ney."

She may have been a pretty girl if she smiled. Kind of Irish with dark red hair, some freckles on a round face, a slightly turned up nose. Instead, if anything, her frown deepened.

"I know you too," she said.

"You're mad at me."

"I'm not mad at you."

"You are. What did I do?" I asked.

She looked at me with cold, green eyes. "You made my boss angry."

"He take it out on you?"

"He took it out on everyone within three blocks," she said. "And on half the port as well, if you must know."

"Ouch. I truly regret that. I do."

The redhead shrugged. But she gave me an idea.

"Let me make it up to you," I said, putting on my best smile. "Have you eaten?"

"It's all right."

"No. It's not. Let me buy you lunch. The least I could do."

"I couldn't," she said.

"Sure you can," I countered.

"I don't think my boyfriend would like that."

I doubted she had a boyfriend. Girls always came up with that excuse when they felt they were getting conned by a fella. I always wondered why.

"He can come. Does he have a phone?" I said. "It's only lunch. Really."

"You're a gangster."

That wasn't nice. Once I bootlegged. Had I stopped being that? "Is that what Ney told you?"

The girl nodded.

"He has it wrong. I work for Coastal Register and Supply."

"Gambler then."

"We supply slot machines, sure enough. But other things, too. What I do is honest work for honest pay." That was partially true, sort of. At least it was before they took Papa Regelo away.

She considered my honest Paddy face a moment. "I'm no quiff and the bank's closed."

Okay, she was no easy piece and there wouldn't be 'accessible' today.

"It's just lunch. Swear."

She surrendered to the free food.

"I usually eat at The Diner. It's right up the street."

"Let me do better. How 'bout The Outer Reef? An extra block and around the corner." The Outer Reef was three steps fancier than The Diner. At about three times the price.

"The Outer Reef?" She looked impressed.

I nodded. She shrugged.

"Let's ankle." I smiled.

The Outer Reef offered seafood with an Italian twist. I guessed that by the heavy garlic fog filling the street for a couple of blocks.

Red and white checked table cloths. Small, pink roses in tiny crystal vases. Little white candles, in matched crystal holders, left unlit. Wine bottles in shadowboxes on the walls. A black-suited, oil-haired host to lead us to one of the few open tables. To hand us menus. He pulled out the girl's chair and slapped open the folded napkins to place them in our laps. This startled and impressed me. The girl took it in stride.

"Anything to drink, Miss? Sir?" he asked.

She looked at me. "Tea, I guess."

"A drink drink?" I said to her. "Anything?"

"You mean wine?" she asked.

"It'll probably be served in a coffee cup, but yeah."

"Scandalous," she said.

I looked up at the host. "Let's choose our food, and we'll have whatever you recommend."

He smiled and nodded, as if I had done something right. My momma taught me to defer when I was in strange territory.

"Impressive, gangster," she said.

I held my hand out over the table.

"I'm Connie Miles. They call me The Conner." Being called a gangster got old after a while.

"Hello, The Conner." she smiled and took the offered hand. "I'm Rylie Dowd. I'm not going to tell you what they call me because I don't like it."

"Tell me. I promise not to call you that."

"No," Rylie said and our waiter appeared, saving her from being pressed for it. "The sea bass."

The most expensive thing on the menu. I smiled and nodded, trying not to swallow hard at it. I took the snapper.

"You don't mind? The bass, I mean," Rylie asked after the waiter disappeared into the kitchen.

"Not a bit." The lie came easy enough, even as I did a quick mental inventory of that wad of bills in my pocket. "I figure your boss threw one righteous fit."

"He did. All of a sudden everything had to be done yesterday. Why hadn't I done this? Why not that? Wishing a lot of people to perdition."

"Including me, I'll bet."

"Especially you, Mr. Miles. What did you do to him?"

"What do you think I did to him?"

"I know you accused him of what happened to Mr. Godines. And I wondered why."

Our lunch brought a cloud of garlicy steam. The snapper was good. The chef knew how to grill fish. And the pale green wine, he called it Vinho Verde, and brought it in coffee cups as predicted, went well. Another guess on my part. At the time I didn't know anything about wine.

I let us eat in what I hoped was a friendly silence. Rylie wasn't about to let me off the hook, however.

"So?" she asked.

"What?"

"Why did you accuse my boss of that?"

I scratched at my cheek to give myself a minute to sort out my words.

"Mr. Godines was a longtime customer of my company. We want to know what really happened to him," I said.

"That's a job for the police, isn't it?"

"Do you really think that man they shot killed Godines?"

"I really don't know."

"My bosses don't think so. They asked me to look into it."

"Why You?" Rylie asked in obvious disbelief.

My chuckle bubbled up no matter my effort to stifle it. "Truth to tell, that's sort o' what I thought. An assignment's an assignment."

"And your way to look into it was to stomp into Mr. Ney's office and accuse him of murder?" Rylie whispered the last few words, eyes darting to the people near us.

"Honestly, just asking didn't work. I thought pointing a finger might rattle him some."

"Did it?"

"Scare him? You tell me?"

"I've never known Mr. Ney to be scared of anything. Especially not of any..." she started, then politely not giving over any rude descriptions.

I gave her one. "Not any two-bit hood?"

"I did not say that."

I took a bite of fish. Rylie looked down at the table cloth. Maybe I didn't scare Ney, but I made him mad. I had to decide. An explosion of an innocent man, wrongly accused? Or a guilty one?

"You know, Rylie, he could've done it. Maybe he had reason," I said.

"What reason?"

"I was hoping you'd tell me. I know they argued over the Port of Houston."

"Not in front of me, they didn't. I never saw them exchange a cross word."

"Well, I still think Mr. Ney had reason. Don't know if he had the time to do it, though." I hoped Rylie would pick up that hint. She didn't. "Do you know where your boss was the night Mr. Godines died?"

"I don't offhand. He's a busy man. Most nights he has to attend some function or board meeting." Rylie gave me a glare. "Is that why you got me here?"

"Hey, if you don't know, you don't know. I'm just paying you back for the grief I caused you. I swear. Somebody'll know. Just have to keep asking."

"You've asked other people?"

"Of course."

She continued with the long look, but I guess she bought my story because she relented some. "I know where you might find out, if you need."

"Yeah?"

"Yeah. The library," she said.

"You're kidding."

"I'm not. Somewhere there's a write up about him. It'll list everything he's a member of. Look those things up. When they meet. Find out, then you'll know where he was. He never misses a meeting. Might even have a story in the paper about it and who was there. You could read a book while you're about it. Be good for a man like you..."

I only half listened. A man stared at me. I caught him out of the corner of my eye. He looked away. Didn't recognize him, but he knew me. I was sure of it and a cold knot grew in my gut.

Rylie misread the change on my face.

"I really didn't mean anything by it, The Conner," she said.

"No, no. I took no offense. I just got to thinking of something else," I said. Time to talk about something else as well. "Tell me, how did you end up in Galveston?"

"Raised here, actually. My folks came down from Fort Worth when I was a baby..."

I let her tell me about herself but I really paid little attention to what she said. My eyes kept returning to that man and to the two men he sat with. Both were businessmen. I could see that he made efforts not to be caught looking at me.

The three of them finished their meal, rose, and left. I avoided his eyes as they circled us and headed for the street. I was relieved when our waiter brought a couple of dewberry ices to our table.

"Know him?" Rylie asked and took a bite of her dessert.

"You noticed?"

"I did."

"No, I don't know him. He knew me though," I said. "Did you recognize him?"

"No. But I know those two other men. Well, not know them, but I've seen them before. They come to our office."

"Yeah?"

"Yes. They work out at the Cotton Exchange. Our company arranges shipping for them."

Great. The Cotton Exchange. Up Broadway a mile or two. Town Gang territory.

The man stood on the curb a block up when Rylie and I left the café. I stopped and gave him a pointed glare. He just stared back at me.

"That's scary. I don't think I'd like it if you looked at me that way," Rylie said, at my elbow.

"If he can do it. I can do it."

I walked Rylie back to her office, right up to the elevator.

That awkward moment descended upon us as we waited.

"Thank you for having lunch with me," I managed.

"We're square, okay?" she asked.

"I hope so. I'm sorry I caused you a bad day."

"I'm pretty tough for a girl. And I know how to manage Mr. Ney. Most of the time."

"I had a good time. It was nice."

"It was, for me too," Rylie said as the operator levered the Otis opened. "And, The Conner if..."

"Just Conner."

"And Conner," Rylie said. She stepped in the elevator. "You ever stop being a gangster..."

The operator gave me a puzzled frown and closed the door on her unfinished sentence.

I'M SHOT

If I decided to stop being a gangster, then what?

I really wanted to get that elevator back and ask Rylie what she meant. An offer of promise, or the start of another reprimand? Instead of calling back the Otis, I stood and stared at the closed door.

Nothing like ginger curls and warm eyes to turn a fella's head. On that day it was not what I needed.

I tried to shake it off. To remain alert as I left the building. No one familiar walked the street. I started toward the Studebaker, then thought better of it. I'd already been chased in that baby. Once bitten, twice shy. A meander might do better. Here and there. Up, down, and around.

Took the time to check store windows. Paid more attention to what the glass reflected than to the displays. I did random, but found myself ever closer to the port.

I figured if I could work down past the old Moody Cotton presser, and the couple of industrial stock fields, then over to Post Office Street, I could get back to the car. I would see anyone that followed me.

A stroll past the cotton presser on the road was — well, it was just that. A stroll. Cutting through the field that held racks of iron rails was a muddy affair. Shorter, with the primitive walkways made of rough-hewn lumber that followed along the stacked rails. Stored for the train station, I guessed.

Threading along on those drooping, rain-soaked walkways worked me like I was doing a circus act. But those unstable planks saved my life. I stepped onto a loose plank. It sagged into a puddle. I jerked back. Something hit iron with the sound of a hammer strike on an anvil. A spray of debris stung the right side of my face.

They'd found me.

I'm shot at, dammit! An instant dive onto the wet grass. Another hammer-anvil clang.

Damn. Damn. Damn. I scrambled, on hands and knees, through a space between the racks. Plopped, butt in the mud and knees up, to lean against the grease-smeared rails.

Another bullet followed, to clang off a rail and whine into the sky.

Trapped. Knew I was dead. Knew my last moment would be face down in bloody muck. And I didn't even know where the bastard was.

Something warm trickled down my jaw. Blood. It dripped onto my mud-streaked jacket.

The stacked rails gave fair cover from the shooter. If he stayed put. The second row blocked me in. If the man changed places, it'd be like being trapped in a tunnel.

I wanted to run. I would run but there was a thousand miles of nothing in every direction beyond the shelving.

Christ, I'm dead. It ends here. In the fucking, God-damned mud.

What I fear, I hate. Hate grew.

"I will not die crawling on my knees, you shit."

I stood, blind to everything but rage. I pulled Livia's stupid pop-gun. With me because she insisted that I'd go armed. Because it hid easily.

The first shot kicked up a spray of water some forty feet in front of me. Miles from the weedy hedge where I thought the gunman lay. Aimed higher, sky high, the second shot made no splash.

Someone screamed. A harsh, animal scream. Me.

A third shot. Somehow I began running at him. Howling.

The man popped up out of the scrub, rifle held across his chest. He stared at me like I was crazy.

Now. It ends now. Damn, one final curse to fate. I fired again.

The man ran. Ran away. Why the hell did he do that? I couldn't have scared him. Not with the belly gun. Someone else yelled.

"Conner! Conner!"

Bobby Lee spattered across the grass. He came up panting, drooling, laughing to beat all.

I made a quick glance at the man carrying his rifle on down the block at a trot. "What's so goddam funny?"

"Ya – you," he managed. He held out his pistol and rocked back and forth. A march in place. "Rahhh!" pant, pant. "Raaarrr. Raaarr. Bang. Raaarrr. Bang. You and that little toy charging artillery."

"What are you doing here?"

"Followed you, o' course. Manny's idea. Couldn't let you go skirt chasing off over here all by yourself." He paused. "You want to go after that guy?"

I didn't.

Manny showed up a couple of minutes later, having tried to head me off downtown. He'd heard the rifle fire and came on the run. He grabbed my chin and gave my face a rough check.

"Looks like you got a load of rat shot right in the puss. You'll live, though," he shook his head, disgusted. What was he more disgusted with, my bloody face or the fact that I was going to live?

A couple of hours later, I sat on Livia's couch, clean and in dry clothes. Dr. Kennedy stood over me, picking bits of crap out of my face with large surgical tweezers.

I winced, neck cocked left so Kennedy probed, picked and pinched. More blood trickled down my cheek. The doctor pushed at the towel crammed around my neck, to catch it before it ruined another shirt. Missed. My last good shirt stained red. He dug into my face again.

"Damn, Doc," I complained.

The tweezers appeared close to my eyes. They held something black and bloody. A tiny thing.

"Iron this time," Kennedy said. "Cup?"

Bobbie Lee pushed forward one of Livia's tea cups. He'd spent the last half-hour peering over Kennedy's shoulder. Fascinated, as Kennedy dropped the bit of iron in the cup. And he still wore that stupid grin on his face.

Again with the prod and probe. Again the winces.

"I will never use that cup again," Livia said. She'd made a pointed effort to avoid her couch. She leaned against the sink and sipped whisky from another of her tea cups.

"That's what we got soap and hot water for," Manny put in. He haunted the open door, not all that eager to watch the surgery himself.

"There's not enough hot water and soap this side of the Bay to make me use that again." Livia turned to pour herself more whisky.

Doc hurt me again. I grimaced.

"Sorry," he said.

I was more embarrassed than in pain. Bobbie Lee had taken every opportunity to tell his story of my suicide charge across the sloppy field. I heard rumbles and chuckles coming from Manny's crew out in the hallway. I was sure they talked about me.

"All right. 'Bout done," Kennedy said. He thumped my swollen lower eyelid. "That bit's staying, I'm afraid. Too close to the eyeball. You can just say it's a beauty mark."

Bobbie Lee sniggered. "Like you ain't pretty enough already."

"All right, my beauty, now's the pain part," Kennedy warned.

He leaned down to fish out some gauze pads and a medicine bottle. A dark, rust-colored liquid spread through the gauze as he slopped crap on it. Mercurochrome.

I groaned. When he daubed my face, I hissed like a raped cat.

"Damn, Doc!" I croaked through a bigger grimace.

Kennedy took hold of my chin and twisted my head this way and that. More daubing, but this time with clean gauze. I saw dots of fresh blood show on it.

"If you liked that, try this on." Kennedy pulled a white, pencil-shaped object from that bag.

"A styptic stick?" I moaned. Barbers used that to stop bleeding from nicked chins.

More sting. Another grimace. My cheeks ached from doing that. My neck ached from Kennedy's need to torture my wounded face.

"Here, hold this," he said and pressed a large gauze patch to the side of my temple. He then wrapped a long strip of bandage around my head, over the crown, across the gauze patch, under my chin, and back again. "Leave this on tonight so you won't seep on your pillow. Take it off tomorrow. Let your skin breathe. Dry out. I'm leaving you some mercurochrome. Dab it on three or four times a day."

"You got it, Doc."

"I'm leaving some laudanum, too." Kennedy looked up at Livia. "A tablespoon now, girl. No more. Another when he wants to sleep."

Livia nodded from her spot against the sink.

"You'll live," Kennedy said to me.

"I will?" I returned. Didn't feel like I would.

The Doctor shook his head with a half-smile. He packed his stuff and left, not looking back.

Bobbie Lee gathered up all the bloodied debris left scattered across Livia's floor and table, and folded it into a section of newspaper.

"I'll throw this out on my way to the room," he said, cheerful, ready to find an audience to retell his story of the fateful charge of Conner Miles.

Manny stepped over, pulled a flask from his hip pocket, and handed it to me.

"Brandy to chase down that swill Doc gave you. Good stuff," he said.

I nodded thanks to him.

When the two of them were out in the hall, Livia closed the door and came over to the couch. She spooned some laudanum into me.

"Here." I patted a place on the opposite end of the couch.

She gave me a puzzled look, but sat there. I shifted and laid the good side of my face on her lap. Tension drained from me. I felt warm. Comfortable.

We stayed there for a good amount of time, sharing the brandy. Livia tickled her nails lightly up and down my arm. God, did I like that.

"Was she pretty?" Livia asked.

I didn't have to wonder long over who she meant. "Sure, I guess. Pretty enough."

"Pure as the driven snow, I bet."

"Most likely."

"You like 'em like that, huh? Fresh scrubbed and untouched?"

I twisted to look at her over the patch of gauze across my temple. She didn't look at me.

"No. I don't like 'em that way," I said, surprised to find that was true. I didn't like girls like Rylie all that much, didn't care how fetching they were. "The price is usually way too high. Time and effort. And money, for what a guy gets out of it."

Livia looked down at me and smiled.

"I cost a lot too, Conner," she said.

"I know, pretty one. I know." And I knew that was true as well. "More than I could ever afford, most likely."

We were silent for a while. Livia continued to tickle at my arm. I made a purr, a quiet growl, for how good it felt.

"What am I going to do with you, Conner?" she said. Not a question I didn't think.

"Anything you want to," I answered.

She swatted my arm. I scrunched around some, as if to burrow deeper into the couch. Loving the scent of her. The skin of her thigh. The starched linen dress. The light perfume she wore.

The laudanum wafted over me like a warm blanket. My eyes drifted closed. I was aware, kind of, as Livia slithered from under me. I heard her Miles bed lowered and Livia remove the linen dress.

As she slid beneath her sheets, I heard her say, "We will see what we will see, Conner."

THE LIBRARY

Me, I don't sleep deep on opium. An off and on, in and out thing, as if my dreams invade a half-conscious stupor. The laudanum didn't stop the pain, but I sure didn't care if it hurt. Didn't even care that someone's shoe tap-tapped the couch leg.

But it was Manny. With a message.

"Up, Irish. Up."

My groan would have been an obscenity had my lips worked.

"Jesus, what do you want?" I managed.

"I brought the skinny. The straight dope. Just call me the Daily News," Manny said through smiling teeth.

"Livia might not like you barging in her room," I said, bringing a wad of blankets with me as I sat up. Where did they come from?

Livia came around the couch, hand balancing a steaming cup on a mismatched saucer. "Come on, Conner. I let him in. You slept through me stomping around, coffee making, and Manny pounding on the door."

I took the coffee from her, grateful. "So I couldn't still be asleep?"

"No," Livia said. "Manny brought news."

"What's his news?"

"Don't know. He hasn't told it yet." Livia fetched her own cup and sat next to me.

Manny stood over us like a tomcat with a mouth full of canary.

"For Christ's sake, what?"

"The coppers hit Fat Tony's still night before last." Manny's smile was pure glee.

"You're joshing me. They found it?"

Fat Tony's distillery. A legend around town. Folks said it was huge, its location a best kept secret. And it kept the Town Gang in hooch for time out of mind.

"Let's say, they got a bit of help, but find it they did," Manny said. "A hundred gallon tank. Barrels of mash. A ton of sugar. Shelves of empty bottles. Even stacks of labels."

"I, uh... Damn." I had no other words. Giant news for sure. This hurt the Town Gang.

"I know," Manny said. "Do you know what's best about it?"

"What?" Livia asked.

"It got Johnny Jack to agree to a sit down with Mr. Quinn. Any luck at all and we'll be back in business by tomorrow."

"All right. I'm off the hook." Weight drained off my shoulders. Manny lost his smile.

"Conner, you sure it's Johnny Jack putting the spot on you?"

The weight came back. I wasn't sure at all. "Well, it was a Town guy that put the shooters on to me yesterday. I think anyway."

"Not really the same thing. You ain't real popular downtown, for sure. Not since you shot that junkie. Don't mean they put out the hit. Just means they knew you got the spot."

That shut me up good.

Livia laid a warm hand on my thigh. "Not a problem, Conner. We'll just keep our eyes open."

"Small potatoes, my friend. You're tougher. Proved that yesterday," Manny said. Well, what if, next time, they didn't miss? Tough doesn't make a fella bullet proof. "So, here's the word. Don't go charging any cannons."

"What the hell does that mean?"

"That means if folks go shootin' at you, don't be shootin' back."

"If I live, you mean," I said.

"That's right." Manny nodded. "If you live. Today it would be best if you run."

"I will," I said into Manny's doubting eyes. "Run like hell, I swear."

That would be my first lie of the day. If I get shot at, I'm shooting back.

Manny gave me a skeptical shrug. "See you down the road. Don't forget to duck."

"Promise," I said as Manny closed the door behind him.

Livia topped off my cup with the last of the coffee, then came to sit with me. We sipped for a while, listening to the clatter and rumble of people walking up and down the hallway. That and the hiss of rain against her window.

"I've been thinking about Sister Judy today," she said.

"What about Sister Judy?" Whoever the hell that was.

"An old nun I knew at the orphanage. She kept laying hens out the back side of the orphanage. One of my chores, sometimes, was to feed 'em. Here, chick. Here chick, chick. They used to peck my feet. I hated those chickens."

I laughed. "Well, if you miss it, I'll peck your feet."

"Yeah, I bet you would." She slapped my arm. "Anyway, I'm beginning to know what those chickens felt. Being locked up in Sister Judy's coop all their lives. Let's go out."

"Where?"

"Let's go see a moving picture. You want to?"

I didn't really. Going out and about had been risky, thinking on it. But there were places I did want to go. "Make a trade with you."

Livia returned a flirty leer. "What kind of trade?"

"Not that kind. Not this time anyway." I grinned. "If you take me to the library, I'll take you to the pictures."

"The library?" Livia said, incredulous.

"Yeah. The library."

"What's there?"

"Some answers, I hope. Answers I can't get other places anymore."

She looked at me, puzzled. "Why not?"

"Because of me making a hash of this whole damned mess with Ney and Mrs. Godines."

Livia rested that warm hand back on my thigh. And said nothing. I guessed she agreed.

After lunch, we huddled under a borrowed umbrella and splashed out to the Studebaker.

Rosenberg Library had the look of a brick building that had survived the big hurricane. All the opulence of imitation European. All the heavy squat of a government project. The inside smelled of mildew and old books.

The librarian seemed welcoming enough. Only the barest glance at the blotchy mess that was my face. And polite enough to make no comment. He was old and scholarly, with his turn-of-the-century black suit and the pinch-nose glasses hanging from a chain round his neck. His musical Southern accent worked hard on proper articulation.

I gave him my brightest smile. The one I reserved for an opening line to a skirt that showed promise.

"I want to research the town's upper crust. The top of society, you know," I told him.

"Why would you want to do that?" Suspicion crossed the librarian's face.

Didn't really want that question. However, I'd considered it on the drive over. Once a salesman, my mother called him a drummer, drifted through my home town. He wasn't there to schlep door-to-door, but to hustle the area shops. He wanted his company's products, I've forgotten what they were, put on store shelves. I took that ploy. "I got a product I want to sell."

"What product would that be, youngster?" the man asked, his voice, still suspicious, got sort of fatherly.

I hesitated, on purpose. "Sir, I'm not free to tell just anybody. It's a new thing and there are secrets my bosses want to keep. At least for a while."

"You tell your customers, I hope?"

"Oh, yes sir."

He shook his head, bemused at some dumb kid on the hustle. He also took me to a corner of the library and dropped a stack of books on a table.

"Social Registers and recent catalogues of Galveston businesses." He pointed over to a bin. "Newspapers for the last week. Check them, too. If any of our betters held a meeting, it's in there. Over with the classifieds. Often as not, any important person attending will be listed."

"Thank you, sir."

I dug into the most recent, as Livia wandered off into the maze of bookshelves. None of them was newer than last year. Thank God for indexes. Saved me from a mind-numbing, page-by-page search. The Business Registers quickly gave me a peek of Ney's rather far-flung business interests. Sea Way Shipping. The several groceries whose behind-the-counter shelves held Beach Gang booze. And whose isles carried our slot machines. A lady's clothing store. More groceries on the mainland. Two maritime supply shops, one here, one in Houston. A bookstore, of all things, over in Baytown. A trucking company out of Harrisburg. Familiar to me. We used it sometimes to carry liquor up to Kansas City.

Things would have gone quicker, but every ten minutes or so, Livia would appear. She'd wink. She'd blow a kiss. A rolled shoulder and a "come hither" look. Once she hiked up her skirt to flash a knee.

The social registers showed a lot of Ney's after-work activities. He chaired two Boards of Directors, and sat on three others. He was a member of the Galveston Beach Association, which put on the annual Bathing Beauty Pageant. The Educational and Recreational

Community Association. The Community Chest. The Galveston Playground Association, whatever that was. He was counted among the overseers of St. Mary's Orphanage. The Little Theater Committee. He belonged to the Order of Chosen Friends, which I knew gave money to the aged and disabled. He even sat on the Rosenberg Library Board of Directors.

I gained a whole new respect for the creaky chair that held up my sorry butt.

Others showed up on those pages. Sam Maceo showed prominently. He turned out to be a bit of a giver, supporting several benevolent causes. Brother Rose got a couple of mentions. Chief Higgins was a member of the Association of Negro Businessmen and the Brotherhood of Laborers. My darling, Bess Godines, gave her time to several ladies' society groups, some charities. I noted she was on a couple with Ney. The Reverend Love did not participate in Galveston's upper crust's compassionate efforts. My guess was he kept too busy with his church and the men in the white robes.

The newspapers, to my disgust, gave Ney his alibi. On the night Godines died, he spoke at a Rotary Club event that, according to the papers, provided nosh, whatever that was, and music late into the night.

I stared long at an empty spot on the cluttered table as if it was one more dead end.

Livia made another of her little peek-a-boos and saw the look on my face.

"You all right?" she asked.

"Ney didn't do it," I said.

"What clued you?"

I lifted the Daily News. "He gave a speech that night."

"Believe everything you see in the papers?"

"Don't matter. A jury will."

Livia flounced over to me, clutching her purse and causing her dress to sway in a dance of its own.

"I'm thinking Rose and Dianne Starr won't be needin' any jury. If he's the guy, then he's the guy." She pressed herself on the chair. Pressed her middle, warm and firm, against my shoulder.

I looked up at her. "You're a dangerous woman, I'm thinking."

She smiled. "Maybe as dangerous as that lily white skirt that steered you to the library. Let's go to that movin' picture, Conner."

Livia sounded almost jealous. I made no comment.

Buster Keaton's new one, The Seven Chances, played over at the Queen. Livia directed me to the Martini. Its moving picture? Sally, the story of an orphan struggling through life. Great.

I took heart seeing the Marquee. Colleen Moore played Sally. Doe-eyed, Cupid-bow lips, oval-faced, bobbed flapper Colleen. Right easy on a man's eyes.

On thinking about it, Miss Moore did kind of look a little like Livia. Livia without the curls. Maybe that brought us to the Martini.

Of course, I was wrong.

We wedged our way as close to the center as Livia could get. The pianist entered to spotty applause. As he began to play and the screen flickered with the newsreel, Livia drew up her skirt and pulled a flask from a garter. We scandalized the couple next to us by sipping whisky through the news bulletin.

Jews were being attacked in Berlin and across Eastern Europe. A lynch mob remained camped around the Dallas County Jail, trying to get at a Negro accused of murdering two men and attacking two women. To brighten things up, selections of our Bathing Beauty pageant glittered across the screen. Half-shy young girls in their swimsuits pranced and posed, liking the camera's attention. Crossed-legged girls smiled as bespectacled old men judge ankle, shin, and knee. The winner turned left and right to smile over alternating bare shoulders.

We lucked into a Felix the Cat cartoon. My favorite.

Sally, it turned out, washed dishes at a restaurant. She had her sights set on a better life. Her dance teacher landlord taught her ballet. Seeing her potential, a customer fixed her up with an agent who set her up as a fake Russian ballerina. At a fancy reception, that customer saw her and fell in love. Sally turns him down since the fool did not love her when she was a lowly dishwasher. She went on to become a star, but the customer persisted to finally win her over.

True love found a way, I guessed. Stupid plot, but I probably would have done the same. Colleen had great legs.

Livia's eyes glistened when the movie finished. Maybe many orphaned children had similar dreams. My heart broke a little. I became ashamed of my glib thoughts.

SOUR LAND

"Sour land. Sewer land. I don't got-dahm care," Rose Maceo spat.

"Saarland," brother Sam repeated patiently. He pronounced it Zar-land. "Saarland Properties."

"I dohn friggin' care. Can't do bid-ness wid 'em."

I didn't care either. I got hoisted from a second hour of sleep the day after taking Livia to the moving pictures. Then drug to this breezy vacant lot by Manny. Apparently to watch the Maceo brothers argue.

While the movie screen flickered, the Beach Gang made their peace with the Town Gang. Livia and I found the Palace Hotel empty except for a couple of guys hulking over piles of belongings and my Netrodyne. Those guys made sure we had all our stuff – and only our stuff – and helped load it in the Studebaker. They waved goodbye and the two of us spent most of the rest of the night stowing everything and airing out my flat.

Then Manny came calling and drug me into the sunshine to watch my bosses argue in front of a couple of terrified marks. One of them in a brown suit too small for him, sporting Ben Turpin mustachios, with his belly lopping over his belt like a sack of rice. The other lanky and as pale as an undertaker, sporting Buster Keaton glasses and sweating in the wind. Mutt and Jeff looking for the gates of Hell to open.

"I got men working on it. They'll come around," Sam reassured.

Rose waved a dismissive gesture. He turned to the marks. "We gotta deal, right?"

"The lot is yours, Mr. Maceo, sir. At the price you offered," the fat one said. He dug at his collar.

"I tink a lil' less den dat," Rose said.

"Yes, Mr. Maceo.'

"You hear from dat Sewer-land bunch, you come to me."

"Yes, Mr. Maceo."

"Good," Sam said. "Now, why are you two still standing here?"

That was an invitation to leave if I ever heard one. The marks turned and fled.

The Maceo brothers exchanged a glance. Both nodded at the sad humor of it all. Then Sam turned his eyes onto me.

"So, Conner, you good?"

"I am, Mr. Maceo. Thank you."

Rose stepped up to me. His strong hand took hold of my jaw. He turned and twisted my skull, staring fiercely at the wounds on my face.

"Near healed up, mah fren. Dat's good."

"Much better, sir." His concern flattered me, but I was glad when he let go. About twisted my head clean off my shoulders.

Rose continued to stare at me with flat eyes. "Foun dem boys dat shot at you."

Boys? More than one? Christ. I nodded, trying not to seem surprised.

"Yeah," Sam Maceo put in. "The good Reverend Love ratted them. Strange, don't you think?"

"Hmm. Yes, I do."

"Aren't you thinking he might have done it? Might have got Godines?"

I shrugged. Shook my head. "Love and his bunch woulda lynched him. Burnt his house down. That's more his style, I think."

The two brothers exchanged another glance. And, maybe half a smile.

"My bra an' me been havin' da same thought. Dat's good, yeah," Rose said. "Looka, you wanna see dem fellas dat shoot at you?"

"It's my mess. Let me know where they are. I'll clean it up, too." I didn't relish what I'd have to do. "I'll go see Love, too."

"Uhh, you know what, Conner," Sam said. "Let me and Rose deal with it. Those men belong to folks we don't want to upset too much. Anyway, we think Love came to us with this as kind of a peace offering."

"What? They're not his men?" I asked.

"They're from out-of-town. Came in trying to make a few bucks. Didn't know who you were."

I took a moment. Sam Maceo seemed well-informed.

"You've already dealt with it, I guess."

Sam nodded. "Put 'em on a train last night."

"Did they say who put the spot on me?"

Sam shook his head. "Open contract."

I hissed an obscenity.

"Who dat did Godines, you tink?" Rose asked me.

"Frank Ney, most likely. Can't prove it though."

"You ever ask him if he whacked Godines?" Sam asked.

Couldn't keep the grin off my face. "Down right told him he did it."

Another pregnant glance between brothers.

"What did the man do?" Sam raised an eyebrow.

"Popped like a pinched tick."

Rose laughed. A pure, happy laugh.

"Good, dat. Good, good, mon cher," he pronounced it 'shaa'.

Sam did not laugh. "Can we be sure he did it?"

"I am sorry, Mister Maceo. I am not totally sure. I can't see a real good reason he had to."

"Who else has a good reason?"

"His wife."

"Betrayed?"

I nodded.

"Embarrassed?"

I nodded again.

"Can you see her doing it?" Sam asked, peering close in my eyes.

"A woman like her, in the dark, at a whorehouse? I have a hard time seeing it."

"You tol her dat she did it" Rose asked.

"I did." I said. "Popped like a tick."

Sam waved his brother silent – before he could laugh. "Dianne Starr. Go see her. She's a touch impatient."

"I'll go there soon as we're done here," I said.

"Go tomorrow. There's some mucky-muck soldiers come in for some kind of training. She's entertaining them tonight."

"Tomorrow, then."

"Not too early."

"Yessir."

"I must go. Have some generals and their wives to entertain myself. The Opera House. A casino or two. Cocktails with too much sugar in 'em." Sam shook his handsome head. "Nothing more boring than a gaggle of generals' wives. Good luck to you, Conner."

"Thank you, Mr. Maceo," I said to the back of his head as he walked down to the Bentley and the two thugs standing beside it.

Rose Maceo smiled. The affable smile of a friendly neighborhood barber, just like he started out in life.

"Wha' cha tink 'bout my lot?" he made an expansive gesture over this patch of scrub grass, sand, and thistle.

"I like it," Manny said. "Nice view of the water."

"Well placed, too," I nodded vigorously. The Hotel Galvez, Murdoch's Pier, and a couple of bathhouses up the road. Some fishing piers down the road. The lot wasn't far from where that Mexican couple cooked up their stews.

"Putta hotel here. Sto' too, maybe." Rose let his eyes drift skyward. I could almost see his vision, myself. "Conner, come see."

Come see what? Manny nudged me and whispered. "He means come over here."

Where was here? Rose strolled toward the traffic on Seawall Blvd. and the beach.

"Podna," I thought he meant partner. Flattering. "How do you feel?"

"All right, Mr. Maceo." I answered.

"My eye. Getting shot at. Dat's no good, no. I don like dat. No dom good. How you feel?"

"Pretty shaky, truth told."

"Trut told, yeah. You wanna kill dem bastards. I'd wanna kill dem bastards, me. You?" Rose turned a hard eye my direction.

"Yeah. Kill 'em." There was nothing else to say.

"Can't do it, mon cher. We got bid-ness wit dem bosses. You gotta be all right wid dat. You all right wid dat?"

I shoved my hands in my pockets. Nothing else to say about that either. I nodded.

Rose nodded back.

"I tank on dis. I tank and tank," he said. "I tank maybe a Lutin is on us. You know Lutin?"

A Lutin, he pronounced loo-tan. What the hell was a Lutin? I shrugged and shook my head.

"A Lutin is a dead baby ghost. A not baptized baby ghost. Dey play tricks. Get cruel sometimes. You tank?"

"As good an answer as any, I think," I said.

Rose laughed. "Maybe so. Maybe not. I don know, me. Could be Godines' ghost."

"What?" I asked and regretted it immediately. I didn't think Rose Maceo would like being questioned.

Instead he laughed again. "I knew dat man. A little. You know dat man?"

"Not really. I mean I never met him." I noticed that his thick accent softened some.

"You know he liked dos colored girls?"

"Yessir."

"Maybe all doz angels up high be all blondes like in dem museum. Maybe he come back down here. He be a joker, him. Be like dat man to stir things up."

"Could be. My life's stirred up, for sure."

"Ohh, shut my mouth and call me coo-you." Rose made an exasperated gesture.

Coo-you meant foolish, stupid. Heard that from some Cajuns that had our slot machines in their stores. I sure wasn't agreeing with my boss on that.

"Conner, I don think all is as it seems." Rose put his hand on my shoulder. On my shoulder. "I'm not what I seem. Dat's one of my secrets. Now maybe you know dat."

He was right. Came as a surprise, but I realized it right then. That accent going away some.

"You go home," he continued. "You think on things as dey seem. Maybe they're not dat. Drink whisky. Let gettin' shot at get outta you mind. Yes?"

"Yessir," I said. And that's what I went to do.

I had Manny drop me at the grocery store. Figured to walk home from there. Thought the walk home would do me some good. Give me time to shed stuff off my mind.

A can of beans. A can of peaches. A half-pound of ham slices in a fold of wax paper. A loaf of dark brown bread smelling good. Three bottles of ginger beer. I even bought a chunk of chocolate from Holland. The smiling, portly grocer still in his stained butcher's apron dropped all of this into a small crate the ginger beer came in. I appreciated his generosity and said so. He got to keep the coin change.

Galveston Island breezes can be friendly in early summer days. I liked the way the gentle wind danced across my arms and fluffed at my hair.

Still could not shake off the memories of bullets singing over my head as I quivered in the mud. That horrid day rolled through my mind over and over, like a newsreel gone crazy.

This was not what Rose Maceo meant, I didn't think.

Closer to my place, I saw some kid, maybe sixteen, trying to mow the lawn of a cottage-style house. His push mower took foot-long bites out of the lawn before the grass fouled the blades. He'd back it up then plow it forward again, and again. I could hear him growl.

"Grass got too long, huh?" I called.

"Think so, do you?" he spat. "No. Sorry, mister. Mad at the mower, not you."

"Don't worry about it. Kind of know what you're dealing with," I said. I did too. I kept biting at being shot at and making no headway with it. Not unlike the kid's hand-high grass. "Just keep at it, you'll get it done."

The kid shook his head. "Yeah, maybe by July. Thanks, though."

I gave him a nod, shrugged at my crate of groceries, and chugged on.

As I entered, Livia sorted through the small stack of records she had collected. Some New Orleans blues already thrummed from the Victrola. Bobbie Lee sat at his usual place on the floor, a scrap of board between his feet. He tossed his knife in the air so that it flipped once and fell to stick its point in the board. They turned to me.

"Well?" Livia asked.

I just rolled my eyes and kept on into the kitchen with my crate. They trooped in behind me as I put the ginger beer into the ice box.

"Damn," I said. "We gotta get more ice."

"No. No, no, no, Paddy. You're not passing on this," Livia complained. "What did they say?"

"Sam and Rose were bitching about some land deal. Some idiot was trying to sell some beach lot out from under them. They were having none of it. Scared that poor sot half to death.

"That's all?" Livia arched an eyebrow, her face more angry than curious.

"Rose took a good look at my face."

"And?"

"He agreed that getting shot at is a bad thing."

"Rose should know," Bobbie Lee put in. I ignored him.

"Told me to get over it," I said.

"You might find me agreeing with him," Livia said.

"Not all that easy."

"I know, Conner. I'll do what I can to help."

"Thanks, Livia."

"Not enough, Paddy. There's more."

"No, there's not."

"Never play poker. I read you like a newspaper."

A sigh escaped me. A surrender.

"Dianne is getting impatient. I gotta go see her tomorrow afternoon."

"Dianne said that?" Livia asked. I shook my head. "Then who did say it?"

"Sam. Rose. I forget," I said.

Livia's face went all puzzled. "Not Dianne?"

"She wasn't there."

"If one of the Maceos said it, then it's the Maceos that are impatient."

"Damn," Bobbie Lee swore. "Not who I'd want impatient with me."

Me either, frankly. "Rose also went on about some kind of swamp ghost."

"The looties or something?" Livia grinned.

"Yeah, the Lutins. You know," I said. "That's something like what Manny told me when he was hauling me home. Said he thought the Maceo's are bothered about things."

Livia came over close to me. "Manny may be right."

"Hey, we get to go see the Handmaiden," Bobbie Lee smiled.

Livia stirred through the pantry and straightened up holding one of my bottles of Irish whisky. She handed it to me. "Grab a glass. Sit on the couch. Do like Rose said. I'll make lunch."

I spent the afternoon brooding. Half aware of the sandwich and ginger beer. Half aware of Bobbie Lee leaving and coming back with a block of ice dripping all over the floor. Half aware of Livia listening to the Victrola as she stood staring out the window. More than half aware, however, of cringing against cold steel, my butt wet in the mud. Of the hammer sound of lead smashing into iron rails. Of my stinging face.

Sometime after dark, the only thing I was over was my empty bottle. A couple of vengeful gulps of laudanum sent me to bed.

A toss and turn stupor. In a sweat. A person would figure a double dose of liquid opium might get him over just about anything. It just got me into a dream. Almost familiar, canyon-like, neighborhood streets, one after another. If I could make this block and that turn, I'd be closer. Didn't know closer to what, but I'd be closer. I'd take that turn. There'd be another canyon of an almost familiar street, and another almost familiar turn. And, I would be closer. Only there waited another street with a turn at its end.

Something touched me. I sat bold upright.

Livia sprang back. "Easy, Conner. You all right?"

"Jesus. Dream."

"Some dream."

"Don't remember much. I tried to get home. A long way to go. I was lost."

"Well, you're home and I made coffee," she said.

"Good. I want some." A lie. Livia's coffee ranged from brown water to black soup, depending.

Bobbie Lee and I left midafternoon, with Livia's promises to keep the door locked, to let no one in, and to keep her little belly pistol close. Whoever hunted me hunted me, or so I'd convinced myself. I figured she should be safe enough. That's what I hoped anyway.

The Handmaiden's brothel appeared quiet, though the old ex-boxer guarded the porch as usual. Nice job if you could get it. When we'd topped the steps, he'd retreated behind the vine-covered trellis that gave discreet cover for customers.

"We need to see Miss Starr," I said.

"She's not here," the man rasped.

"I was told she wanted to see us this afternoon."

"Zat so?"

"It is."

He considered us a moment. "Told me dey expected one guy to come see 'em."

I glanced at Bobbie Lee.

"Don't worry. I'll stay here. Maybe some of the girls'll wanta dance or something."

"Or something," I said. Bobbie Lee shrugged a shy grin. "Want some money?"

"Nah, I'm good."

The old boxer waited until he disappeared inside before he turned to me. He jerked his chin toward a house across the street.

"Dat's Mary's Fordson out front," he said.

The truck, 1922 maybe, shone and glittered in the sun, fresh waxed and pristine. Mary had to have a lot of pride in it. I doubted it ever did duty as a work vehicle.

She opened the door of the solid, red brick house that was handsome more than pretty. Like Mary.

"Conner. You good?" she greeted.

"I am. You?"

"Can't be better. Come on in." She wore black slacks, patent leather men's pumps, and a white dress shirt – not tucked in. Suspenders dangled loose down her legs. Puffy eyes proved her late night.

She led me through the entry to a parlor on the left, filled with aged, utilitarian furniture. That the room showed doilies, crystal lamps, and antique portraits, surprised me. I expected art deco or something. Dianne, the Handmaiden, sat regally on the settee, a cup of coffee in her hand. She wore a simple, severe, black dress that contrasted with the décor. I sensed she'd worn it the night before. The sun, shining through the window, gave a halo to her blonde locks and accented the cherry colored birthmark on her cheek.

"Miss Starr," I said, entering the room.

Dianne put her cup on its saucer and came to me. "Hello, Irish. How are you?"

Her smile, full of concern and curiosity, was not unlike Rose Maceo's as she scrutinized my wounded face.

"I'm healing up. Slow but sure."

"Good. Good. I'm about ready for some Scotch. Want some?"

"Yeah, I would."

Dianne shot a glance at Mary. Moments later, the tall, taciturn woman put a glass in each of our hands.

"So, Conner, why are you trying to get yourself killed?" Dianne asked.

"Christ, does everybody on this God-forsaken island know about that?"

"Everybody," Dianne confirmed. "What came over you?"

"Don't have any idea. One minute I cringed, the next I was all in a sweat over something so damn dumb."

"You know, Conner, stuff happens to people. Somehow some kind of button gets pushed. A nerve gets tickled. Something just comes over a person. Happens to us all one time or another," Dianne offered.

Inside me, something fell into place. I wasn't quite sure what but I could almost hear the thud.

"I had that happening to me that day. For true." I shook my head. "But I'm not trying to get myself killed."

"If you say so. Tell me then, who's trying to kill you?"

"I'm pretty sure it's Frank Ney."

"You're only pretty sure?"

"Yeah. Can't figure out why, though," I said.

"Some people don't need any big reason, Paddy," Mary put in.

"We'll get back to that," Dianne said. "Tell me who killed Peter Godines."

Dismayed, I shook my head. "I've really bent the axle on that. I'm sorry."

Dianne gave me that concerned smile again. "Sit down, Conner. Take a breath. Take a drink. Then you can tell me about it."

I sat on a lumpy loveseat, took that breath, and took a drink.

Dianne sat on a lounge chair opposite me and put her half-finished drink on a marble-topped end table.

"All right. I feel it's either... Well, I think... Mr. Godines' wife has the best reason to kill him. But I can't see her doing it. I wouldn't put anything past Ney. But I can't see Godines' death profiting him any."

"Mr. Ney is all about lining his pockets. That's a fact." Dianne grinned.

I perked up. "You know him well?"

"Oh, not really. He has come to me to provide company for some businessmen visiting Galveston. Every now and then." She must have noticed my shoulders slump. "You're disappointed. Why?"

"Miss Starr..."

"Call me Dianne, Conner. We're friends enough."

"Dianne," I said, flattered she considered me a friend. "Where I messed up was making the two of them mad at me. I need to know more. They won't talk to me."

"What more do you need to know about them?"

"About Peter, really. What he was doing with his money."

Dianne chuckled. "He was spending wads of it on women of easy virtue."

I laughed in turn. "His business money. Especially in the weeks before he died. And I'd like to know more about how he acted around his wife. Other things, maybe."

"But, those two aren't talking to you."

"They are not."

Dianne looked at me. Almost harshly. I was reminded again of Rose Maceo and the way he looked at me. She brought up a fist and thoughtfully knuckled the birthmark on her cheek. Unwanted thoughts about her magic hand came into my head. I couldn't help it.

"I might be able to help you, Conner. I can try. Let me get back in touch with you." Dianne said.

—————

ARSON

—————

BOBBIE LEE SLEPT. CURLED UP ON MY FLOOR. HE PREFERRED floors, waking or sleeping. I wondered if he slept on the floor of that pitiful shack he grew up in. Hell, I wondered if he slept on the floor in his room at the boarding house around the corner.

Livia came out from my bedroom with a sheet. She dropped it over him. The night was warm. The sheet would probably start him sweating. A nice gesture anyway. She went from there to turn down the radio. A California station we picked up somehow, broadcasted a real good swing band.

"Come on. I'll buy you a drink." I walked toward the kitchen. She followed. I chipped ice as quietly as I could so we had the treat of Irish whisky on the rocks.

"What do you think Dianne's gonna fix up for you?" she asked.

"No idea."

"I wager you that it will be something, if I know the woman."

"I think I'll pass up that bet." I reached across the table to lay a hand over one of hers and looked into her eyes. "It's time, Livia. I need to know."

"To know what?"

"You know what," I said. "I need to know what you are not telling me about the night Peter died."

Livia looked back at me. Inside she struggled. I saw it on her face.

"I promised, Conner," She answered finally.

"What did you promise?"

"I promised I would not tell."

"Who?"

"Conner, please don't ask me that," Livia pleaded.

"You must. Don't you think Peter is due? We owe him."

"I don't owe him, Conner." She pulled her hand from beneath mine.

"For me then. Tell me for me," I implored.

Livia looked down at the half-full glass of whisky. She reached to take hold of it. Forever passed. Or maybe a minute.

"Peter was still alive when I got to him. He stared up at the sky, blinking. He gurgled and panted. Bertie came from the house. Peter had requested her..."

"She came from the house? Before he was stabbed?"

"Bertie came after, Conner." Livia sounded sure of it.

If I decided to believe her, I wouldn't be forced to reconsider protective brothers and cousins of the pretty Negro whore. I wouldn't be forced to go back to Chief Higgins. Anyway, I liked Bertie. She was a good woman. True-hearted, by all that I could see.

"All right, after," I said. "What happened with Peter?"

"His blinking." She shook her head. "I can still see him staring at the sky, blinking. He seemed to notice. He looked. At me. At Bertie. He reached out his hand. To Bertie. She sat down beside him and took it. I sat on his other side. We were with him until the end. Only a few moments. I try not to, but I hear his last breath."

I watched a single tear make its way down her cheek to her chin where it clung. My finger came up to touch it. To draw it off. To put it to my lips and taste the salt of it.

"I'm sorry, Livia. I'm sorry for Bertie as well."

"She made me swear to tell no one. She was afraid of anyone knowing she was there."

"It's still her secret. I swear it to you."

Livia reached for my hand this time. The same hand that had taken her tear. "I'll hold you to that, you stupid Paddy."

"Let me buy you another drink."

"Several, I think."

We were drunk and sloppy when we tiptoed past Bobbie Lee curled up on my floor. His snores were soft and breathy.

I stripped down to my shorts and Livia to her bloomers. I only remembered that because of what came later. Sleep, drunken sleep, swept over me like the humid breeze that eased through the open window.

The dream put me in the grass and nettles back from the beach. The old Mexican couple sat across the fire from me. They gave me the secrets of their stew recipe. In Spanish, and they knew I couldn't understand them. It frustrated me. I had a headache. For some reason I knew the pain was real, outside of the dream, as I slept.

"Christ. Christ. Jesus bleeding Christ. Conner. Conner. The damn house is on fire. Conner!"

The dizzy pain whirled the world as I sat up. The air choked. "What?"

"They're burning us man. Wake up!"

All I could do was cough. Bobbie Lee seemed a wraith. A specter standing in the smoke-filled dark. I felt Livia sit up in a fit of wheezing.

"Come on. We gotta get out of here," Bobbie Lee yelled, shrill and hoarse.

I don't remember how I got my pants on. I remember Livia, draped in a sheet, grabbing a fist full of her jewelry with one exposed arm.

"Save the radio. Please," she begged.

I went out and got it, not thinking how silly it seemed. Livia had her priorities.

"Hurry, goddammit!" Bobbie Lee yelled again and again.

Hurry I did, barefoot, in nothing but my pants, and all bent over as I tried to see around that damn speaker horn. Livia right behind me.

I tried the front door. An acrid billow of smoke swooped over and around me and caused tears to flood my eyes. Livia banged against me as I stopped short.

"The back! The back!" I yelled.

Another awkward effort to twist the knob and hold onto the radio to get into the kitchen. Another to open the back door. Thank God, the back stairs were clear of smoke and flame. Down I went as best I could, all the way to the grass.

A man stood there staring at me. Little more than a shadow against the flaking paint of my building. His hand held a gas can.

"Well, hell, you woke up. Bad for you." He pulled a huge pistol from his belt.

I stood there. Stupid. Stunned. Knowing that tonight I would die.

The man, with hard purpose, thumbed back the pistol's hammer.

But he faltered. His hand trembled. His arm dropped. The pistol slipped free. And the man fell on his ass. Puzzlement on his face in the red glow of spreading flames. The gas can tumbled free, spewing gas in an arc across the grass.

I saw something protruding from where his shoulder met his neck. Bobbie Lee's knife. Bobbie Lee bumped passed me, ran over to put a foot on the man's pistol and wrenched the knife free. I turned away as he plunged the knife into the man's throat.

"Jesus, Bobbie Lee, Jesus," Livia sobbed.

"Sorry, darling. Had to make sure." Bobbie Lee dragged the blade across the grass to clean it. He smiled up at me, lurid red in the fiery glow. "I don't think we should leave him here."

I put down the radio. "Drag him into the house. Let him burn in his own damn fire."

My heart had no sympathy for the bastard that scared me so bad.

Bobbie Lee made a quick glance at the house. "We should hurry, I think."

The two of us sucked in a breath, grabbed up the dead man, and heaved him to the door of the empty downstairs apartment. I had to drop him and kick open the door. I limped for days. Another damn breath to get the body into the building.

When we came out, I caught sight of Livia hauling the radio toward the front of the house, the sheet barely covering her. We followed.

Bobbie Lee leaned close to my ear and whispered. "I got his pistol. Give it to you later."

Damn, I left mine inside.

Neighbors gathered in the street. In the distance, the fire truck bells clanged insanely, coming closer.

Took three days to feel like I halfway recovered from the fire. Days of borrowed clothes, shopping for more, and spending money I didn't really want to let go of. Days of taking bath after bath and still smelling of smoke.

Livia shook all of the first day and took all of the second for her to be able to even look at Bobbie Lee. He felt really bad about it, apologizing ceaselessly to the back of her head.

Manny came to move us back into the Palace Hotel. Livia in her old room, with Bobbie Lee next to her and me across the hall. A handful of families, come to play in the surf, shared the floor with us. How I didn't love the little ones tromping up and down the hallway, early and late. I like them being there anyway. Less chance of trouble.

Like before, I spent the third evening in Livia's apartment listening to the radio. Only that night, I nursed cold beer in a hot sweat. Livia kept a cast iron fry pan on the stove, heating two hand irons. She took turns with them, pressing our clothes.

"Thanks."

"Thanks for what?" Livia asked, pounding that iron on one of my shirts. I hoped she'd not char this one like the one tossed over in the corner.

"Thanks for doing my clothes." And for the smell of hot cotton, as I enjoyed the sight of her bending over the ironing board.

"Aw, shucks cowboy." She laid on a country drawl. "Can't have you going 'round like no farmer, now can I."

"Guess not." I might have been walking around all wrinkled, but my shirts wouldn't have been burnt.

The radio station cut away from the orchestra's attempts to do some jazz and went to a New York feed so everyone could laugh with W. C. Fields.

"Get some music out of that thing, if you can?" Livia asked.

I went over to twist the knobs, making the box squeal and sizzle.

"Conner," Livia said before I could find something. "Conner."

"Yeah, what?" I said, finding a swing band.

"I hear somebody knocking on your door."

As fast as I got to the door, pistol in hand, Livia was quicker. I went back against the wall. Livia cracked the door opened an inch. She puffed her relief.

"Manny. Hi. He's in here." She opened the door.

"And, I'm in here." I heard Bobbie Lee say. He must have heard the knocks as well. I'd give even money he held his pistol.

Manny came in, took a look at me, and grinned. "Ready for trouble. Good."

"Heavens, Manny. It's been days. How are you?" Livia gave him a hug, which he returned, wrapping her up with his strong arms.

"Too long, girl," he said. "I'm good."

"Well, come on in. A drink? Coffee?"

"No time, darling. I gotta borrow your fella for an hour or two," he said looking at me with a sharp gaze.

"Dianne?" I asked. I hoped.

"Rose."

Damn. I really wanted her to get me close to Mrs. Godines and Ney.

"I'll stay with Livia. We'll be all right." Bobbie Lee slipped in and held the door just as two little boys clopped past to the end of the hall.

I caught their wide eyes, half full of curiosity, half full of fear of adults.

Manny turned to them and made tickling motions with his fingers. "Get cha, get cha, get cha."

The boys fled, squealing, back to their parent's room.

The sappy grin on Manny's face was a marvel.

"Really?" I asked.

"What? I like little kids. Plan on a passel of 'em one day."

"Really," I repeated, a statement more than a question.

"Yeah. Bet on it."

"I'd bet you'd make a great daddy," Livia said, as Manny led the way out.

I followed and imagined Manny as a father.

He drove me to an area of warehouses not far from the port. A dingy one in particular, but not particularly dingy, set in the middle of many equally as salt worn warehouses. Enough paint remained on the sign that I could make out Quinn's Restaurant Supply. The only things a café could get from this shabby hulk were slot machines.

The front office had everything I could want in a used couch and a beat up desk. And the butter on the corn – the hugely despondent Reverend Hollis Love sat forlorn on that dirty couch.

The good Reverend stared at me, wordless, not even angry. I sure didn't speak to him. Manny didn't give him a nod. He just led me through the maze of crated slots stacked three deep, that smelled of sawn pine, excelsior, and damp cement. The echoes of our slapping shoe leather and being lost in the dim sameness, for some reason, made me dizzy.

There was an open space toward the back. Three men stood in it. Part of Mr. Maceo's inner circle. Dangerous men.

Two other men sat in wooden chairs. Rose Maceo sat in one, feet planted square, hands tucked under his arm pits, and a dark fedora shadowing his eyes. The other man in the second chair, his face was pale, his curly hair tousled and hung onto his forehead. He was dressed in his shirt sleeves, and his dark eyes stared at the floor.

"Mr. Maceo," I greeted. Manny took his place behind Maceo and leaned against a stack of crates.

"Conner," Rose said. His chin indicated the man in the other chair. "You know dat man?"

The man looked up at me briefly, hate in his gaze. Fear was in it too. But not at me, necessarily. He didn't seem beat up or anything.

"No, sir," I said.

"He knows you. Don't cha, fella?"

The man did not move.

"Sorry. I don't know him." I shook my head.

"Tell the Conner here where you're from," Rose said.

Without looking up, the man mumbled. "Kansas City."

Memories of a dark night on an empty road in northern Louisiana reeled through my brain. Three cars blocking our truck full of corn liquor. The dim, angry faces of men holding guns. They told us they were from Kansas City. The singular memory of a pistol shot. A shot I fired. And a dead man. The first man I ever killed.

"Damn," I spat. "Is that why people want to kill me? Is it?"

He remained silent.

"I'm sorry, Mr. Maceo. I told Conner this thing was handled. I thought it was." Manny straightened up.

"If it wasn't before, I think it is now. Right, Kansas?" Rose asked. The man nodded. "Say it out loud, Kansas."

"He wasn't part of the Beach when he killed our man," Kansas said softly, without looking up.

"You unnerstan, mah fren, dat now dis man is part of da Beach?"

"I understand."

"Conner, take a look on dis man," Maceo ordered.

I did.

"You'll know 'im if you see 'im again?"

"I will," I said.

"You see 'im again, you don't have to let me know. You just take care of it." Rose's words were pregnant with meaning.

"I will." Saying so didn't stop the cold knot that gripped my gut.

"You unnerstan', Kansas?" Rose asked. Without waiting for a nod, he looked at me. "Go on wid you."

I was dismissed. Manny and I left. Behind us, I heard Rose.

"I go ahead and freight that shipment up to your bosses. You tell 'em they're welcome," he said.

Hollis Love still sat on that couch when we got up front. I went and sat next to him.

"Reverend," I said.

"Mr. Miles."

Mr. Miles, now I liked that. I nodded toward the back of the warehouse. "This another one of your presents to the Maceos?"

"I guess you could call it that," he replied.

"My question to you is, how in the hell did you know anything about this?"

"One of my parishioners, a widow lady, has a boarding house. Some guys got a room there. Guys from out of town," he said without looking at me. "She doesn't trust much of any of what she calls foreigners. But one day she caught one of 'em coming in all in a sweat and carrying a rifle. One of her neighbors had a phone. She gave me a call. Called again when this one came looking for his friends."

I thought for a minute. I'd lay odds she saw that man on the day I cowered and listened to his bullets pass over my head. I'd also bet that those men never made it back no matter what I'd been told.

"Well then, I guess I owe you a thanks, Reverend," I said.

For the first time he looked me in the eye.

"I appreciate that, Mr. Miles."

CRUSHED STRAWBERRIES

SOMETHING BLOOMED SOMEWHERE. THE COOL MORNING BREEZE brought the sweet scent to me. Well, cool compared to the damp warmth of my room. Bobbie Lee and I sat in the best of the cabanas between the Paradise Resort's block buildings. I listened to the arid rustle of the palm fronds as they struggled to give us shade. The shrill hum of the mosquito trying to find my ear. The calling gulls.

"They sound sad, don't they?"

"Who?" Bobbie Lee asked.

"The seagulls. Like they've lost something precious."

Bobbie Lee laughed. "Maybe they went and found it and it wasn't as great as they hoped."

I couldn't help smiling at that in spite of not wanting to.

"More like," I agreed.

"You got a whole batch of Irish luck, my friend. I can't believe Rose Maceo did all that for you," Bobbie Lee said.

"Do what?"

"Squaring you with Kansas City. Twice. Holding that shipment up for you. While you were gone, Livia and I went walking on the beach..."

"That was a risk, Bobbie Lee."

"Well," he did a how-could-I-help-it gesture. "What can a guy do? Anyway, a bunch of our boys wasted the day over by Murdoch's Bathhouse. One of 'em told me they had four or five freight cars, loaded and ready to go, just sittin'. Rose wouldn't..."

"Mister Maceo," I reminded.

"Yeah. Right. Mr. Maceo wouldn't let 'em loose. That cost money. He doubled down on you, man."

"Not really, I don't think. I'm not that important. The Maceo's are defending their, or rather, Ollie Quinn's castle."

"Castle?"

"Their home ground. Their territory."

Bobbie Lee brushed his hands together as if to slap off dust. "Two, four, six. Done is done. Simple."

"Simple," I agreed.

Then Bobbie Lee got a look on his face. "Maybe too simple."

"Maybe."

"Think we should still watch our backs."

"Think you're right."

Having that thought tightened me up. I didn't appreciate it. The flowery breeze on the sunny morning had been a comfort. For a while.

"If she stabs you, I'll shoot her," Bobbie said out of nowhere.

"What?"

He gave a nod toward our building. Livia and Contrary Mary walked toward us. Livia in a filmy, ivory linen summer shift. Contrary Mary in her overalls and barefooted. Today she chose to wear a man's white shirt under it. They carried glasses of a red liquid. Two each.

"Thought ya'll would like some refreshment." Livia smiled. "Lime juice and crushed strawberries."

"I got uncles down on the border near McAllen. They ship stuff to me." Mary shrugged a shoulder.

Well, at least the trains from the south were going through, the

Maceo's or not. The stuff was pretty good. Tart enough to pucker everything from my lips to my eyelids, pulpy with those crushed strawberries, and sweeter than my virgin sister's best friend. I wondered if there was a spoon full of sugar left in this whole block. It'd wake a person up, but it was nice enough that pleasant morning.

With the girls – no, don't think Mary would like that – with the women sitting opposite us in the shade, Livia made it her job to engage us all in proper conversation. Summer celebrations planned for the Island. The places – the proper places – we'd been to in New Orleans.

I enjoyed watching her play hostess and suspected that some of her schooling at the orphanage showed through. She started – tried – to talk the latest fashion for men as well as women.

Contrary Mary spoke. "Dianne's got ya'll set up to meet Ney and that Godines woman. The Galveston Playground Association yearly gala. You boys have good suits, I hope?" Mary asked.

"Got it," Bobbie Lee said.

"Think so," I hedged. Was mine all that good?

"Don't think so. Don't guess." Mary glared. "Have a good suit."

"I'll take him shopping," Livia said. "Get him set up knife sharp. I swear."

Contrary Mary, who knew something about blade edges, smiled. I wouldn't want her smiling that way at me.

"Make sure you take the trip, Conner," Mary ordered.

I nodded.

"Don't worry, Mary. He'll come," Livia said.

"Why don't you go bring us some more of the juice?" Mary asked.

"Yes, ma'am."

"I'm nobody's ma'am, Livia."

"Yessum. I'm going."

"Help her out, Bobbie Lee." Mary shook her head.

Bobbie Lee didn't even nod. He just got up and trailed after Livia. Mary's eyes followed them until they were out of sight.

"All right, Irish, what do you want with our two friends," she asked.

I knew the friends she meant. "I want to know how Godines was really spending his money. Not his paycheck. His investment money."

"Why?"

"Because it might point to why he was really killed."

"Not the woman scorned?"

"Scorned. Maybe. But, why now? What would it serve? She as much as told me her bed had been empty for years. She didn't seem to care. Not that much, anyway."

"And she would know about his money?"

"Maybe. Maybe the bank accounts are reachable. They traveled around the same circles. Spoke to the same people."

Mary considered that a couple of seconds, then made a pass-on-by tilt of her head.

"And, Ney? I think you told us they were fighting."

"Disagreeing really. On what direction their company would go."

"The disagreement, as you call it, got hot?"

"Warm. Ney's got a short enough fuse, true. As far as I know, Godines never sank company money in his interests. Same with Ney. The company just kept on doing what it was doing."

"These feelings of yours may change if you learn more about what Godines was buying?"

"They very well may, yes."

Mary made another of those gestures. "All that laid aside for a moment, who did it?"

I shook my head. "I seriously don't..."

"You're so full of Irish sheep shit, Paddy. Who do you think did it?"

"Ney." A pure guess. I was not sure.

"Because he's trying to have you killed?"

"Rose Maceo found all that out. People coming after me for my misspent youth."

Mary stared at me and kept that gaze until Livia and Bobbie Lee returned with a pitcher of lime and strawberry froth.

"You boys get yourself ready for high society," Mary told us. "You have until Wednesday. I'll send Manny to pick you up."

"We'll be ready," I assured her.

"Oh, yeah," Mary added. "Where you're going, Dianne is going as a business woman. So you call her that. No mistakes."

"Yes, ma'am," came out automatic. Couldn't stop myself.

Got the glare. Swallowed hard.

DESSERT

"Yes, Miss." Albert, my tailor at the busy Strand Men's Wear, kowtowed to Livia as she instructed him.

"And the gray as well as the navy blue, I think," Livia added.

"Yes, Miss." He knuckled his pencil mustache amid the fog of Bayberry scent and the garlic of the restaurant next door. All the while, the well-used tape measure flicked and squirmed over my body. It reminded me of the tails of lizards I used to capture in my hands as a boy.

"No problem having them both ready on time?" she asked.

"Not a bit, Miss. I'll get my best people on it."

Livia placed the stack of assorted ties, handkerchiefs, socks, and cufflinks she'd picked out onto the counter. "I'll leave you with it then."

"Wait. You're leaving?" I asked.

"Albert's got you. You're in good hands. Isn't that right, Albert?"

"Measure twice, cut once, Miss Livia," Albert intoned.

"Where are you going?"

"To spend your money, of course," she said over her shoulder as she headed for the street.

Sigh. I looked down at the patchwork collection of fabric I wore. Albert assured me he would magic it into a suit. His tape measure flicked and slithered as he used some strange bit of stone to put little marks here and there on the cloth. Every so often he would stop and stick a pin to it.

"Mind the pins, sir," he would say.

I stood so still that I shuddered. No pins stuck me, though I could feel them.

"There now. Done," the tailor said.

Finally.

"Did you measure twice?" I teased.

"I surely did, sir."

"So you only have to cut once."

Albert smiled. "Yes. Only once, Mr. Miles."

"I'll look forward to wearing them, Albert."

"You'll not be disappointed. But, be careful changing out of it."

"The pins?"

"The pins."

I stiff-legged into the changing room and stripped off carefully indeed. Changed into my own clothes. Shot the breeze with Albert a while. I was happy to see Livia coming back, loaded down with packages. Before I could relieve her of her burden, Albert presented me with packages of my own.

"Shirts, and hankies, and such?"

"And such," Albert said.

"What do I owe you?" I asked.

Albert gave me a wink. "I'll add it to Mr. Maceo's tab, as I was told to."

"Rosario?"

"Salvatore, sir."

"He told you to do that?"

"No, sir. Dianne Starr told me to do that. She called me on our new telephone. Quite miraculous, those telephones, aren't they?"

"Miracles," I affirmed, but hoped Sam Maceo would be all right with the charges.

I still worried about moving around town, so I hesitated at the store entrance. Left and right, the sun-drenched street seemed safe enough. But this was Town Gang territory, even if the truce held.

Poor Livia, laden with twine-tied, brown paper-wrapped boxes, looked like the back of a mailman's van with legs. Nothing to do but charge ahead. The two of us hobbled into a Galveston summer morning. Oven heat, air you can wear, humidity causing instant sweat.

"Beach," a muffled echo from the stack of boxes.

"What?"

Livia did a half turn, as much to see where she stepped as to talk to me. "Let's pick up a picnic lunch and something to drink, and you take me to the beach."

Sounded good to me. Right then it did, anyway. "You don't know it, pretty one, but we are already there."

I took her back to the Palace to drop off our packages. Livia wrapped a chunk of ice in newspaper and placed it in a cloth sack. She followed that with a jar of lime juice, sugar, and somebody's homemade vodka. I tried to look forward to going blind from someone's homemade booze.

A greasy spoon called Markem's, boxed up a lunch for us. A wax paper sack of fried chicken thighs, a jar of cabbage salad, another of dilled red potatoes, and one of berry cobbler. The cook was good enough to throw in some paper plates, some little wooden spoons. Two bottles of ginger beer came with it.

No public beach for Livia. We drove south down Sea Wall Boulevard until it ended.

"Farther," she ordered. "Farther."

We passed the last of the beach houses.

"Farther."

"Much farther and we'll be axle deep in salt water."

Livia looked around. She gave me a bit of a smile. "Here will do."

There was a distance – a preoccupation – in her gaze. I hadn't noticed it before.

An uneven line of tangled seaweed marked the high tide level. I backed the Studebaker well up above it but kept short of soft sand.

"This is wonderful, Conner. Let's sit for a while," Livia said.

I followed suit and watched Livia as she looked, wide-eyed, out at the Gulf.

"What?" she asked.

"Just liking the view."

She pointed at the surf. "That's the view."

"No," I pointed at her. "That is."

Livia giggled. I was glad I caused it. But she popped open her door to stand tiptoe on the running board. I got out the other side, propped my elbows on the roof of the car to watch her eyes as they swept the horizon.

"Is that one of your boats?"

A lone steamer, almost to the horizon, slogged her way toward the Bay.

"You mean that ship?"

Livia shot me a glare. "Boat. Ship. That thing floating out there all by itself. One of your smugglers?"

"No. You won't see any of 'em. They're all out about thirty five miles that way." I gestured off south and west. "Rum Row. Figure on about fifty of 'em. All waitin' on us. Us and our money. It's quite a sight. Especially after dark."

"You've been out there?"

"A couple of times. Kind of like a farmer's market. They're all strung out in a long line. We're all swarming along them in our speed boats. They all call out what they got. We're all shouting what we want. Everybody haggles until they're hoarse. It's something, I tell you."

Livia stepped off the running board, came up to the front wheel, and shimmied onto the hood. She threw a leg over and mounted it like it was a horse. Her eyes closed.

"The wind feels good," she said.

The sea breeze wisped her hair and stirred her clothes.

I went forward five or six steps and let it waft over and around me. It did feel good. When I turned back to her, she watched me, mischief in her eyes and in her grin.

"I bought new bloomers." Her smile broadened. "Wanta see 'em?"

Before I could even nod, she grabbed her skirt and lifted it. And there were her stockinged legs in all their glory. Cute bloomers. White with blue stitching decorating her ruffles. The wind reached to flutter those as well.

"Damn, woman. Why do you do this to me?"

She dropped the skirt and giggled. "Because you appreciate it so much, of course. Let's go wading."

She swung a leg over the hood, kicked off her shoes, and went about removing her stockings. I went about appreciating that process. She watched me and laughed.

I rolled up my pant legs then kicked off my shoes.

We were in Texas in June. The water was tepid. Livia had me in one hand and her skirt hem in the other. Splashing along with her on the empty beach made me pensive rather than happy. Her body walked with me. Her mind did not.

I didn't question it. Not out loud. Not when we got back. Not when we laid out a blanket to eat our chicken and drink her sugared concoction.

At the end of it, Livia screwed the lid back on the jar, stuffed the meal's debris back in its box, and stood before me.

She reached up under her skirt and removed her new bloomers.

"I'm dessert," she said.

For reasons I couldn't understand, I knew this was the last time I would make love with her.

We entertained the gulls and one puzzled sandpiper until I spent myself like a nickel in a slot machine. All that time, Livia's eyes never met mine.

"Pleased?" she asked. Her eyes finally reached me.

"From the top of my head right down to the thank you ma'am."

"Pretty damned pleased, myself, if you want to know." She laughed and rolled off me to straighten her skirt and stare at the sky.

What better thing is there for a woman to say to a man? I almost smiled as I adjusted my pants. Livia slung her arm across my chest. Her invitation to have me tickle her skin.

That damned sandpiper, bored with it all, gave me one last, skeptical glance and skittered off into the surf in her eternal hunt for tiny crabs.

"You coming to that Playground meeting?" I asked as I drug my fingers along her arm.

I felt her shrug.

"Maybe I'll see you there." I said.

"Maybe you will, Conner."

ART DECO

"Champagne not a week out of Marseilles, shrimp off the boat not six hours. Russian caviar. Italian goose liver foie gras. Juniper-smoked Swedish eel. Argentinian beefsteaks. The bacon-wrapped scallops are the best things on the bar." The spruce, starched server said, indicating each item with a wave of the hand.

I nodded, stuck for words. The only things he said that I knew were goose, beef, and bacon.

"No Irish whisky?" I asked. He shook his head. I took the champagne.

The Galveston Playground Association's fund raiser rumbled noisily in the ballroom down the hall from the space Manny took me to.

The room, deep in the Magruder Hotel, stunned me. The bar itself was teakwood, shiny and reeking of lemon oil. At each end, the gold-leafed torsos of naked women reached up to support a canopy of smoked glass. Behind it a surreal painting of Islamic castles. Two areas of gold fabric couches and lounge chairs, each surrounded large tables of teak and glass. The ceiling was a great dome, back-lit around its edge, with a circle of Grecian women painted in dancing poses.

From the ballroom down the hall, an orchestra, sloppy and indifferent, played sloppy, indifferent dance music.

In one of the seating areas, Rose Maceo and Ollie Quinn, of all people, sat in conversation with an overstuffed potato of a businessman, in rumpled brown and wearing a white straw boater hat.

Ollie Quinn, boss of all the Beach Gang. A marvel.

I swallowed a big gulp of the champagne and regretted it. The three men ignored me. Thank goodness.

In the other area, Sam Maceo sat on a couch with Dianne Starr, business woman. Still the Handmaiden to me. They looked up at me with big smiles. Vultures on a stump.

Sam's gesture invited me to sit in one of the plush, golden chairs.

"This is really something, Mr. Maceo." I swept the room with my flute, glad at the end of it that I didn't spill any. "All this just for me?"

Dianne smiled. "Thought we'd want some privacy."

"Feel the pressure yet?" Sam asked with some mischief on his mug.

I shuddered. "Mr. Maceo, I do. I don't feel like an ol' country lad the likes of me belongs in a place like this."

"I have learned, Irish, that a man belongs where he makes himself belong."

Sam Maceo, on the surface, was all tailored, buffed, and ritzed. But those burnt-flint eyes were steel hard as he looked at me. The man didn't have to make himself belong to anywhere. He was born belonging anywhere he damn well wanted to be.

"Never seen the like," I marveled. "That inlaid wood around the door. And, Jesus, those lampshades. They belong in a church in New Orleans or somewhere."

"Art Deco," Dianne remarked.

"What?"

"The style of decorations. Of architecture around you. They call it Art Deco," she said.

I decided not to ask who "they" were. Anyway, I got distracted –

big time distracted. Contrary Mary came in the room. And I didn't even believe what I saw.

A man's tuxedo, deepest black, tailored to her long, slender body. Her boyish – no, her mannish haircut, slicked down, shone with hair oil. Makeup of all things. Some kind of pale foundation made stark contrast to ebony eyeliner and dark, near black, red lipstick. Angry eyes swept the room to settle on me for a fair portion of eternity. She marched over to the bar to fist a flute of champagne, then backed against the wall, vigilant.

Manny turned from giving her a once-over. "I'd call that some Art Deco."

"Why don't you and Bobbie Lee go down and get some dancing in," Sam said.

I heard something kind of lively seeping through the wall. Horrid band, but the music would get the Flappers' arms aflapping. Pine Top Smith. Pine Top's Boogie Woogie. Raised a shout, though.

Manny and Bobbie Lee headed out.

Sam looked over at Ollie Quinn. Ollie stood. So did Rose and the Potato Man.

"Got to call it. I wanta see what you got." Quinn put out his hand, to be seized up by plump fingers, glittering with heavy gold rings.

"Fine. Fine," Potato Man said with clipped barks. "Just remember what I told you."

The man faltered. "Well, the words of that damn Yankee banker. If the streets run with blood, buy property."

Quinn chuckled. "Should work for me then."

"Sometimes. Maybe." Rose said. "Still, I'm glad dat damned war be over."

"I tell you, sir, somebody's got to get a handle on those gangsters around here." Potato Man shook a finger.

Rose and Quinn shared a glance.

"Yessir," Quinn said. "Somebody sure does."

The fat man huffed his way out of the room, Quinn right behind him.

Something fell into place for me. Wasn't sure exactly what it was. Fell so heavy I figured everyone in the room heard the bang. The implications made me furious. This mess, all of it, was about Ney buying land.

"Oh, yeah. You were trying to buy some land out on the beach last time I saw you," I said to Sam. "Did that work out?'

Sam buffed his hands back and forth a couple of times, as if knocking off dust. "You saw those two stupid marks?"

"I did. Dirty britches scared."

"Easy as getting a slice of Mom's mincemeat pie." His eyes turned serious. "Tonight's the night to get it done, Conner.'

I didn't have a chance to answer.

"Looks like we're all here." Ney walked into the room like he owned it, with Bess Godines by the elbow. Dora followed behind. He looked at each of us in turn. Me last. "All the interested parties, as it turns out."

We all stood like good Southern gentlemen. Including Dianne. She and Sam moved to offer the couch. Opposite me.

Mrs. Godines passed by me as if we'd never met.

Dora didn't. She squared in front of me and glared. "Looks like they forgot to take out the trash."

"Dora," Ney interceded. "Some champagne wouldn't go amiss. A glass for yourself as well."

Sam introduced everyone, naming Dianne last.

"Miss Starr, is it?" Ney said. I could tell he knew exactly who she was.

"Yes, Mr. Ney. I'm glad you came." She held out a hand.

He took it up with a smirking grin.

Rose came up to join our circle. For a moment we sat looking at each other.

Ney finally spoke. "It's your party, folks."

"Yes. We are concerned about Peter's death, Mrs. Godines," Sam said. "You have my sympathy, ma'am."

"I'm sure," she said, not sure at all. "What would concern you about my husband's passing?"

"Business, ma'am," Sam said. Then he looked to me.

So did Mrs. Godines.

"He the boss that sent you off looking for the man who killed my husband?" She shook a hand toward Sam.

"No, ma'am. Afraid dat was me," Rose said. "I own Coastal Register."

"The police know who killed Peter," Mrs. Godines said.

"Ma'am, that junkie, di Glassi, did not murder your husband," I said, harsher than I'd intended.

"He didn't?" Ney put in. "He died chasing down the one man hunting him for it."

"That right?" My eyebrows shot up. "Interesting."

It was interesting. How did he know that? In the papers the Rangers said di Glassi was caught bootlegging some liquor. It was them that fingered di Glassi for Godines' murder.

"Why don't you believe that, boy?" Mrs. Godines asked. "And why does Coastal Register need to dig around in all of this?"

I ignored her.

"How's the move going, Mr. Ney?" I asked.

"Move?"

"Thought you told me you were puttin' some money up around the Port of Houston."

"Oh, that," Ney paused. To make up a lie, I wondered? "Getting in a little late. Hope the Port grows out to that bit of river bank I bought up."

"Well, I hope you bought it cheap," I said.

Ney shrugged. "Cheap enough, I guess."

Dianne got up, came over, and sat next to me, her eyes puzzled.

"Land's pretty cheap here. For a while, anyway," I said, thinking about that beach front lot the Maceos forced out of the two marks.

"That so?" Did Ney get cutty-eyed when he responded?

"It's what I heard," I said. "Prices went way down when the gangs were going at each other."

I caught Dianne looking at me closely.

"Where are you going with this?" she almost whispered.

"It's the only way some things make sense," I whispered back. Not all that quietly.

"What things make sense?" Ney asked.

I ignored him.

"Mrs. Godines, did you know that the Rangers did not kill that junkie?" I turned on her.

"What's this, Conner?" Sam Maceo asked me as he leaned forward to prop elbows on knees.

"This is cheap land, Mr. Maceo, sir. All of this mess. Cheap land and those that want to buy it," I said.

Ney stood, outraged, or that's the way he looked. "How the hell do you know anything about di Glassi's death?"

"Because I shot him. And it didn't have a damn thing to do with Peter Godines' murder."

Rose also stood. He looked hard at Ney. Like he was watching my back. Maybe he had figured my play. I swung back to Bess Godines.

"Are you having any luck closing out your husband's accounts? Canceling any unfinished or incomplete business deals?" I asked her. She wasn't about to answer. "Maybe you're getting help. Maybe from Mr. Ney."

Her eyes cut to Ney. A brief glance, but filled with unspoken feeling.

"You don't have to say anything, Bess," Ney said without turning to her.

Incensed, she stood.

"I'm not going to. I'm leaving. Dora?"

She stormed toward the door, gathering Dora up as she passed.

Bess Godines was a handsome enough woman, well-constructed.

As was Dora in a fierce storm of a way. I watched them, Ney watched them, as men do. Realization came like the dawn.

It's the hips. Like with Livia. With Ney's secretary, Rylie Dowd. Always the hips.

"I know you killed him," I said.

Mrs. Godines whirled around, skirts twisting about her legs, eyes flaming.

"You dare! Still! Riffraff. I did not murder my husband," she almost hissed through gritted teeth.

"I didn't mean you ma'am." I turned to Dora. "How long have you known about your daughter, Dora?"

The woman grayed. The color of sun-bleached mahogany. No mistaking the anguish on her face.

"Do not speak, Dora. That fool knows nothing." Ney near shouted.

I knew lots. I was getting to know more every minute. She needed a push. "In a parking lot, in the dark, behind a brothel. Were you trying to talk to her? To convince her to stop what she was doing."

A number of emotions washed over Dora's face. The last one? Anger? Resolve? Surrender, maybe?

"I couldn't talk to her," she said.

"Why not?"

A tear seeped from an eye and snaked slowly down her cheek. 'Because I didn't know which one she was."

"So you tried to see if you could recognize her?"

Dora nodded. "I would do that on my off nights."

"And then Peter showed up?"

"Enough," Ney interrupted. "She doesn't need to be speaking to the likes of you. Any of you."

She did, really. I pressed. "Peter?"

Dora stayed silent. At first I thought she took Ney's advice. Maybe she relived that night.

"I couldn't let him."

"Dora, please!" Ney begged.

She held up a detaining hand. "I couldn't let him. Not even by accident. I tried to stop him. He yelled at me. Called me names. Awful names. I couldn't let him. She was his daughter, you see."

A scream. Mrs. Godines. Sam Maceo rushed to her. Took her arm. Probably kept her from falling.

"I'm sorry, ma'am," Dora turned to her. "You weren't to know. I'm sorry."

"Dora, they will put you away forever if you don't be quiet." Ney made insistent gestures with his hands.

"I don't see why, sir," I said. "There are no policemen here. Anyway, like Mrs. Godines said, the Law already knows who did it. Or, think they do."

Behind her, I saw Sam ease the widow into a chair. Behind them I saw Contrary Mary, one hand tucked in the side pocket of her vest. Cold eyes stared at Dora. A hungry stare.

A waltz ebbed into the room. Irving Berlin. "All Alone," of all things. Bess Godines did not yet know just how alone she was.

Dianne came around behind Ney. She fixed her gaze on Sam and tossed her head toward the door. He took her hint, helped Mrs. Godines to stand, and propped her up as he led her out of the room.

Dianne, like the Handmaiden I first knew, turned to me.

"Time to finish up, Conner. Don't you think?"

Yeah. She was right. I was getting tired of it anyway.

"You didn't want Peter dead, did you?" I asked Ney. I remembered he chaired the orphanage governing board. "When you told Dora about her daughter. Where she could find her."

"No. Of course not," he answered. I don't think he meant to.

"Kind of the prize in the Cracker Jacks though, huh? His death, I mean."

Ney shrugged and smiled for the first time. "Yeah, I guess."

Turning to Dianne again, I started. "Come to find out, this mess is not about Peter in the back garden. Or Dora. Or the hair pin that she struck Peter down with. It was a hair pin, wasn't it?"

Dora made the slightest nod.

"It's about Mr. Ney. Mr. Ney and what he wanted. I'm right, aren't I, Frank?"

Ney just looked at me.

"He wanted what Peter had. The easy way was to have his wife." I looked at Ney. "It's why you told Dora about her daughter. Made a bigger mess of her marriage than you thought, huh?"

"That kind of rank bullshit can get you killed, Paddy."

He'd been trying that for a while, I thought. "Then send someone better next time."

"I will," he said before he could stop himself. I had guessed right about di Glassi.

"He wants what you have as well, Mr. Maceo," I said to Rose. I hoped my fear didn't show.

"What's that, Paddy?" Rose asked. But he smiled when he called me that.

"That fat guy, looks like a potato..."

Rose laughed out loud. "Potato. Fits him to a tee. We should call him that."

"Well, Potato clued me to it. Reminded me. That Saarland outfit your people could never find. I thought that name was familiar. You know their offices are in Ney's building. If that bunch had staff at all, they were up in Ney's office buying land you wanted."

Ney's face showed me I was right.

"Looks like dat rank bullshit's yours, you bastard," Rose said.

"Just like you, Maceo, my business has to grow." Ney shoved a hand inside his jacket. "So I think I'll leave now."

Damn. That rat bastard grabbed at a pistol. And I stood there. Jesus, I had to go for him. That or throw champagne flutes at him while he threw lead at me. How far was the leap across that fancy table?

Rose chuckled. Not an ounce of humor in it.

"Dat's duh biggest joke I ever did hear," he growled. "Dere is nowhere for you to go dat is far enough away. You know dat, right?"

"You guys are businessmen," I started. An interruption born of pure, raw fear. Fear of guns going off and bullets flying around my ears.

"So?" Ney asked.

I looked at Rose. "Make a deal. Maybe there's a price..."

His eyes shifted and he raised a preventive hand. I turned to see Sam at the door. Behind him, Manny and Bobbie Lee posed with their look-out-mister faces. I knew they were packing.

Any time Ney wanted to, that gun could let fly. Blood and death loosed down the hall from half the fat cats in Galveston.

Instead Ney, still watching Rose, asked. "A price for what?"

"The price of getting out of here alive," I answered.

"A high price, Frank," Rose said.

"I have a price," And I did too. Or, I thought I did.

Ney gave me the quickest of glances. "What might that be, you dumb Paddy."

"Galveston. Whatever you got here on the Island. Hand it over. Then head for the hills."

"That's not a price, that's a cliché." Ney fished a small .32 from his jacket. But he held it at his side. Thank all the wood nymphs in Ireland.

I had to learn later what a cliché was, but I knew he was interested. If only to get out safely.

Rose looked as if he learned something new about me. "Whatever you call it, I'll make dat deal,"

"Like hell," Ney said.

"Make it or be dead by morning. Nuttin' less."

"I'll be in my office in the morning."

"We'll be in your office tonight. You and me."

"How can I trust that?"

"Keep that little popgun, if you want." Rose shrugged.

The two men nodded. To the surprise of everyone in the room, they left. Together.

I stepped over to Dora. "Go. Leave Galveston."

She looked at me with moist, deep brown eyes. After a moment she nodded. I'm glad she didn't see Mary slip from the room. If Dora got off the Island, I doubted she'd ever make it to the mainland.

Dora's eyes widened. I sensed Dianne ease up beside me. The Handmaiden showed no expression. Cold and hard.

"Go on," I urged the Negro companion. Well, she was no one's companion any longer.

Dianne and I watched until Dora rounded the corner out of sight.

"My, aren't you the Galahad," Dianne said.

"I'm sorry?" Who the hell was Galahad?

"Trying to give Dora a way out, just like the woman had nothing to answer for."

"All said and done, it kinda weighs on a man. I saw Con— I saw Mary leave." Somehow I met her gaze.

"Sit, Paddy. We have some things to talk about."

AN ORNATE FLASK

The Handmaiden went to the glittering bar. She picked up empty champagne flutes and returned to set them on the oversized coffee table.

Then I watched her hike up her dress. A leather holster, strapped to her thigh, held an ornate flask. Like the rest of Dianne, her skin was pale and ruddy. Why was I surprised that a brothel madam had no shame or shyness?

"Bourbon, not Irish I'm afraid. It'll do us, I suspect." She twisted off the cap and emptied it into the two flutes. A lot of Bourbon.

A lot of it got in us while I avoided her gaze.

"You did what I asked of you, Conner. Why does it weigh on you?"

"She's a woman," I said.

"As far as I know, all 'she's' are women." Dianne went on. "Woman aren't due any costs for their actions?"

I shrugged.

"But you saw Mary leave."

It was not a question. I nodded.

"You know that, tonight, Mary is not working for me?"

"I saw her."

"You did. But, Conner, I farmed her out. Tonight she's working for Rose."

Well, damn me for a broke down circus clown.

"Not Dora, then?" I asked.

"It would have been whoever Rose left with. Had you put the thumb on Bess, he would have made to take her home. If Dora, then Dora. If you failed us…"

"If I failed, he'd be taking me home."

She laughed and took way too long to say anything. "I think that, if you didn't find an answer, Rose would be with the two of us drinking my Bourbon.

God, I hoped so.

"Livia Drusilla," she said out of nowhere.

I looked around, expecting to see Livia coming through the door.

"Not our Livia," Dianne said. "Livia Drusilla."

"Who's that?"

"She was a Roman woman. A wife of Caesar."

"Caesar?"

"It's what they called their kings. Honestly, Conner, you need to read a book once in a while."

I'd been told that before. The cute skirt working for Ney. Riley. Maybe I should read some. "All right, kings."

Dianne went on as if I hadn't said a thing. "The poor girl must have been born to be the wife of a Caesar. I don't think her first husband was anything much. Maybe not even her second. Might be wrong about that."

"She was a bit of a climber, I guess." I got an image of Livia in a training gown walking through a crowd of bowing noblemen, on the arm of a king.

The look Dianne shot me made the birthmark on her cheek glow crimson.

"My point is, Livia Drusilla was meant for better things. By the time she died, this Livia was wife, mother, grandmother, and great grandmother to many Caesars."

"This your way to tell me that I won't be seeing Livia – our Livia – tonight?"

"Partly, I think. I'm saying that our Livia is also meant for better things than can be found on Galveston Island." She looked at me. Looking for a reaction maybe. "She did tell me she was sad she couldn't come tonight."

"To say goodbye?"

Dianne nodded.

I didn't believe for a minute Livia said any such thing. But I got an image of Livia, on the beach, being dessert.

"She told me goodbye. In her way. You sent her off the Island."

"No. Her own choice."

"Did you – were you – gonna tell her?"

"About her mother? Her father?"

I shrugged.

"Would you?" she asked.

Another shrug. "She know anything about any of this?"

"Nothing."

"Then, no. I don't think she'd want to know."

"You going to be all right? About her leaving, I mean?" Dianne asked.

"I'm jake. The poor girl had no business with a bottom feeding bootlegger." I saw the denial coming into Dianne's eyes. "I know. I know. I'm better than that. Or, at least, I will be. Still, I got no business latched onto any skirt. Much less somebody the likes of her. Not at this time for sure."

"You better know it," Dianne said.

Not reassured. I did not reply.

"You still running liquor?" she asked.

"Off and on. Rare these days."

"You were working with Papa, right? Collecting from the machines?"

"Whole armies of machines. Piles of dimes and nickels."

"I was sad to hear about Papa. I liked him," she said. "He didn't deserve it."

Wasn't sure about that. Most likely we all end up getting what's coming to us.

"No. He didn't," was all I said.

"You gonna go back to it, Conner?"

"No. I hear there's a crew doing it now. It's for folks higher up on the ladder than me. Maybe like Papa. Too long in the tooth for other things."

Dianne propped her head on her palm again as she slumped back on the couch.

"So what 'cha gonna do with yourself?" she asked.

I turned my head to look out the entry. Spiffy Sam Maceo. Manny with his broad shoulders. Bobbie Lee, still looking like a boy playing dress-up-like-daddy. They stood laughing as the bartender passed them champagne.

I sighed. "I guess I'll be doing whatever Rose Maceo wants me to be doing."

ABOUT THE AUTHOR

Steven D. Malone received a BA in History from the University of Houston. He has been a teacher of life skills and work skills to special needs students, adjudicated youth, and the visually impaired as well as College English. He is a published author and has been a writers coach.

He says of himself: I am a voracious reader of anything from historical fiction to cosmology to the backs of cereal boxes. My interests include ancient and Dark Age history, the Civil War and the American West, Taoist and Buddhist philosophy, and classic movies. I am also a certified teacher of Tai Chi Chuan. In my life I have been a drifter, a beach bum, a library page, a book store clerk, a teacher and a construction worker. Presently, I am a happy husband and proud father.

Visit the author at his website for his previous work, blog, and articles of interest: www.stevenspen.com.

Mr. Malone also asks that you take the time to write a review of the book on Amazon and Goodreads.

www.ingramcontent.com/pod-product-compliance
Lightning Source LLC
Chambersburg PA
CBHW061617100726
47898CB00002B/704